BOY TOY

Dead Husbands Series
Book One

by
K. Wiley Sider

ISBN: 0692224858
ISBN 13: 9780692224854
Library of Congress Control Number: 2014910528
Devilwood Press, Ellicott City, MD

Dedicated to the people who will read this book and wonder which characters are really them.

ONE

Kate called it "The Grenade." Whenever her husband John was stressed or pissed or just felt like sharing his misery, he would make a nasty pointed remark just before closing the front door behind him. It was his parting shot in an already acrimonious conversation and it drove her completely batshit insane. And unfortunately it was the only kind of conversation they were having lately.

With her hand still on the knob, Kate pressed her forehead against the cool wood and tried to calm herself down but her anger continued to consume her with his last comment still hanging in the air around her. What was really unfair was that it gave him the last word in an already uneven argument, an argument that was really about nothing. John had left the grill cover off and it had rained. That's it. But somehow, in John's head, it was the worst thing ever and it was all Kate's fault for not having checked to see if it was on before it started raining. And now his precious grill had water spots on it. Kate shook her head at the ridiculousness of it and fought the urge to grab her phone and continue the argument over text message. It would only provoke John and make her angrier. Instead she went into the kitchen to clean up after their breakfast.

Kate picked up a plate then sank into her chair and despaired for her marriage. It hadn't always been this way though things had been tough for a long time. They had started out like any other newlywed couple with dreams of a bright and successful future. John had just passed his board exams for dentistry and Kate had finished her masters in social work. When Kate found out she was pregnant at the same time John bought his practice, things seemed like they couldn't be more perfect. By the time their second daughter was born, they had found a place to settle down.

It was a pocket community that surrounded a small elementary school that served only those neighborhoods in closest proximity to it. They'd picked the neighborhood for the school and rejoiced in the number of young families that were moving in around them. But though they loved the school, Kate found that she had mixed feelings about the neighborhood. Her street had been added on to an existing community and the older residents weren't thrilled with the addition.

But in time people seemed to move past the growing pains and eventually accept their new neighbors though an unspoken divide between old and new still existed. This left Kate with fewer options for friends among the homes surrounding her. Never one to play the life of the party, she turned to her husband for social support who in turn, to her surprise, turned away.

Now, 5 years later, Kate knew that on John's list of priorities she came in dead last. He'd never been demonstrably affectionate but even the little bit of intimacy he'd mustered in the past had turned into a cold detachment peppered with nagging criticisms about everything from housekeeping to the quality of her mashed potatoes.

She kept telling herself it was stress and that her husband was simply doing what all men did when they were upset about something but displaced their anger onto their wives. It sucked and it wasn't even remotely fair but it happened.

Kate made her mental excuses for John's behavior and felt her sense of calm somewhat restored. She loaded the breakfast dishes into the dishwasher then picked up the phone and dialed her friend Michelle's number.

"Hey," Michelle answered without preamble. "I was just about to call you. You aren't going to the supermarket anytime soon are you?"

"In a little while," Kate replied, "Why?"

"I'm supposed to make cupcakes for Girl Scouts tonight and I've got a guy coming this morning to fix our air conditioning. I don't know how long he's going to be here."

"It isn't even March yet," Kate said. "Are you having hot flashes?"

"Ha ha," Michelle answered. "We were having trouble last fall and there's a deal on service right now. Besides, this is Maryland. Spring only lasts a couple of days."

"Text me a list and I'll pick it up," Kate offered.

"Thank you," Michelle sighed. "So...wait you called me. What's up?"

"Nothing," Kate answered then felt disloyal for calling Michelle to complain about John. "Just another John morning."

"Ugh. Tell me about it. If Dave says one more thing about the laundry, I'm going to serve it to him for dinner."

Kate smiled. She appreciated Michelle trying to commiserate but Michelle's husband Dave was actually a really nice guy who treated his family like they were his reason for breathing.

Rather than argue the merits of Michelle's marital success, Kate played along. "Yeah, it's grill cover for dinner here."

She could hear Michelle snort on the other end then what sounded like her doorbell.

"Oh crap. I think that's him. I'll call you later."

Kate was about to answer when Michelle hung up on her. She didn't take it personally. Michelle had been a great friend since moving just down the street and Kate wasn't about to take her friendship for granted. Unfortunately their conversation was unsatisfyingly short. Still edgy, Kate gave the kitchen a good scrub down then set off in search of something else to distract her until it was time to pick Lizzie up from preschool.

Too wound up for reading and with little left to clean, Kate sat down in front of the computer and pulled up her email. There wasn't much other than the usual school announcements and bids for volunteers for both Lizzie's preschool and Emma's second grade class. She answered what she could and ignored or deleted everything else then went to clean out her junk folder. In case something important didn't make it through to her inbox, Kate scanned the email subjects and deleted batches at a time. Most were either unwanted advertisements or bids for financial assistance from dying third world millionaires. She was almost done when she spied an email from someone named Bethie with a note in the subject line that read "OMG John check this one out." Kate often got emails for John and usually just checked to make sure they were legitimate then forwarded them. She clicked it to open it and inhaled sharply then recoiled in disgust. It was a photo of an erect penis that had been tattooed to look like the head of a snake. *Who on earth would send something like this?* Kate checked the note underneath the photo but there was no name. The only Beth Kate knew of was a woman at their church who was the mother of one of their babysitters. It was unlikely this was the same Beth. With plenty of misgivings Kate forwarded it to John's email then deleted it.

She was still troubled by it when she left to pick Lizzie up from her preschool then at the grocery store for Michelle and was still ruminating over it when Emma got off the school bus that afternoon. The rational part of her knew it was probably nothing but for some reason it was really bothering her. She wondered, given the current state of her marriage, if it was even worth mentioning. John didn't like to be questioned and they were already arguing over minutiae.

They were long done with dinner and Lizzie and Emma were already in bed when John finally got home. Kate stepped into the kitchen to see him sorting through the mail.

"Why are you so late?" she asked with a glance at the clock.

John didn't even bother to look up. "I had an emergency patient."

"Until ten o'clock?"

John made a stack of the envelopes addressed to him then looked up at her. "That's why it's called an emergency."

"You got an email," Kate blurted. "It came to me by accident."

"So? Just forward it," John replied then turned to the plate Kate had left for him on the counter. She knew the chicken was cold by now but she wasn't about to offer to heat it up.

"I did," she said instead. "It was from someone named Bethie. You should know that it was really inappropriate."

"Why are you reading my email?" John demanded.

"It came to my email address. You told me to check to make sure they were legit before forwarding them to you. Who's Bethie?"

"One of the girls in my office," he answered taking a bite of chicken then made a face. "This is cold."

"Of course it is," Kate replied trying to keep her tone even. "We ate four hours ago. Why is one of your employees sending you inappropriate emails?"

"How should I know? You know how those girls are."

It wasn't really an answer and Kate didn't know how 'those girls' were. John kept his work life completely separate from his home life. Kate could count on one hand the number of times she'd been in his office. All she could remember of 'Bethie' was a young and pretty dental assistant named Bethany who was overly solicitous and somewhat prying the first and only time Kate had met her. Kate had chalked it up to youthful enthusiasm and ignored her. In hindsight, perhaps she should have paid more attention.

"I don't think you should be encouraging that kind of familiarity," she said carefully. "It was really offensive."

"Well I wouldn't know, would I? She didn't send it to me."

Kate was about to refute that when John stalked past her and went into his office. She would have followed but knew it would only make him angry.

She watched as his door swung to an almost close then turned to go to bed alone...again.

Nights were tough for Kate. She'd be fast asleep by the time John came to bed but she was a light enough sleeper that she'd awaken as soon as he pulled the covers aside. Then she would lay there in the dark as sleep would slip away and listen to him drop off to into a deep slumber she once had and now envied. Not so long ago he would curl his body against hers and wrap his arms around her. Now the gulf between them was so great she dared not turn to him or she would fall in and disappear forever.

Instead she laid there and stared off into the darkness. She used to talk to God but God had stopped answering and only a thick roaring silence filled her ears and a vast and empty space opened up in her heart.

Love was the blood that filled her veins and without it she was becoming empty, dry and desiccated. She couldn't understand how John could live without affection, yet he did. He could go days, even months without so much as a single touch and not suffer for it at all while she felt like her very will to live was draining away from her.

When she couldn't take it anymore, Kate gave in and got up to take a sleeping pill. She knew she'd be paying for it in the morning but it was the only way to make her mind stop torturing her.

It didn't take long. Thoughts were coming more slowly and with less urgency than before. Then, as she stood at edge of waking before the deep and dark abyss of sleep, she fell.

TWO

It was almost painful to open her eyes. She'd taken the sleeping pill late enough that her tired body hadn't fully metabolized it out of her system. It left her with a headache that only time and coffee could ameliorate.

Kate pushed herself off the bed. It was like pulling out of quicksand. John expected an ironed shirt every morning and she wasn't in the mood for the inevitable argument if it wasn't ready by the time he got out of the shower.

Kate went into the closet and made a selection from a variety of dress shirts then stepped into the laundry room to iron it.

From what she knew of the other women in the neighborhood, no one else ironed their husband's shirt. She'd taken an informal poll last summer and everyone looked at her in surprise when she admitted that she picked out her husband's clothes and got them ready every morning. It was really to help John though. If left to his own devices, he would dress himself like a color blind math teacher from the eighties.

She was musing over her demotion to housekeeper when she heard the shower go off. With the now crisp shirt in hand, Kate carried it into the bathroom to hand to John who was still in his towel, his boxer shorts dangling from his finger.

"I'm getting dressed here. Do you mind?" he snapped.

Kate tried for a flirty tone. "You know we haven't done something, just the two of us, in a long time. I wouldn't mind going out for a little one on one. You could even go like that," she joked nodding at John's nudity.

John hung up his towel then gestured at the air in front of his limp penis. "There you go. You want some one on one, there it is."

Kate stared at him in confusion. "I meant go out...like have a date night. I'm just asking for a little love."

John looked at her with dead eyes. "If you want a little love then you've got to give a little love."

"What are you talking about?"

"It goes both ways," he said as he pulled on his boxer shorts. "You might want lovin' but I want some lovin' too."

"There's a big difference between holding hands and a blow job," Kate protested. She couldn't believe he was equating the two. Since when did he think sex was the same thing as intimacy?

"So it's only what you want," John said flatly.

Kate wondered at what point the conversation had turned into argument. She strongly suspected it was the moment John found the pin for this morning's grenade in her request for a date. Rather than place herself in the line of fire, Kate turned and left the room. She was surprised when John followed her.

"You know, if you want more affection, you could be a little more adventurous," he said.

Kate turned and looked at him. "What are you talking about?"

John shrugged then pulled his shirt on. "I'm just saying, it gets old... always doing the same old thing."

"We don't do anything. Are you saying nothing is the same old thing?"

"No. I'm just saying it would be nice to have something different from time to time."

"What do you mean 'different'?" Kate asked though she already knew the answer.

"You know," John said with another shrug and in a tone that made it sound like he was trying to be reasonable. "Things to watch, stuff to try...different positions, different places...different people."

"You want to have sex with different people," Kate stated.

"Or bring them here...with us. A man needs a little strange sometimes."

Kate took a deep breath. Her face felt tight and the tension that was gripping her head was making her headache worse.

"No normal human being needs to resort to threesomes and porn to have a healthy sex life," she said carefully.

"The girls on the movies seem to be enjoying themselves." John's tone was casual, like he was discussing the weather.

"They are getting paid to seem like they're enjoying themselves," Kate protested. "It isn't real. No one really lives like that."

"All I'm saying is it wouldn't hurt to do things a little different. I can't believe you don't want to try and spice things up a little bit. All you want to do is lay there and do nothing."

Kate hated it when he did that. John was a master at making her sound selfish and uncompromising. More than anything she wanted this ridiculous conversation to end but she just couldn't let it go. It was just too humiliating.

"The fact that you need kinky perverted sex to get off says everything about you and nothing about me. I'm asking you to be loving and you're putting a price on something that should be given freely. But you're not about to accommodate me until I meet some arbitrary and shifting baseline based solely on what you want without regard, or respect, for how I feel about it. That's not how marriages are supposed to work, John."

"Then you must not be serious about making things better," John answered then turned away.

Kate felt the top of her head explode. She knew it was pointless to continue. John was so invested in his warped sense of entitlement that arguing would only prolong the agony. Instead she left the room to get the girls ready for school.

A few minutes later she wasn't surprised to hear the front door close. John had left without saying goodbye. It was just as well since he had left without lobbing another marital grenade at her either.

She put on a smile for her girls then ushered them out the door for school.

Kate spent the day battling her headache. What had started as a sleeping pill hangover had turned into a full blown migraine by mid-afternoon so Kate took another pill and cloistered herself in the dark, windowless bedroom in their basement to rest. She was glad John wasn't home to hector her for being "lazy" as he would put it. Though he often took naps when he was home, he did not extend the same privilege to his wife.

By the afternoon, she was better but felt guilty for having rested the day away. In a frenzy of activity that threatened her tenuous recovery, Kate made her way through the house to give it a cursory cleaning that would definitely not pass a closer inspection. She hoped that it would be another late night for John so that she could give the housekeeping better attention before he got home.

Unfortunately, John was home at his regular time but surprisingly said nothing when he walked in while she was still vacuuming. Instead he disappeared into his office with his cell phone in his hand.

Later that night John emerged in time for dinner and managed to sit and eat with them. Then, when the girls were up in bed, he settled down in front of the TV. Though Kate didn't really care for television, John's being home was a notable enough event that she settled down on the couch with him and feigned interest. Luckily he had tuned in to the History Channel to watch something about ancient aliens. If it wasn't exactly exciting, it was at least interesting. She was so engrossed that she didn't realize that John was yawning in boredom next to her. It wasn't until he stood up and made a beeline for the stairs that she realized he hadn't said a word to her all evening.

Kate stared after him then turned and watched the last minute of the program then turned the TV off and followed him upstairs. When she stepped into their room, she was surprised that he was already under the covers with his face to the wall.

Kate crawled into bed next to him and stared at the back of his head. She could tell by his breathing that he wasn't asleep yet and wondered why he was faking it.

"Is there a reason you're ignoring me?" she asked. She wasn't surprised when he didn't answer. He was fully committed to feigning sleep and this made her extremely angry.

Trying to keep her tone even, Kate tried again. "John."

This time he acted startled and turned his head to look at her.

"Huh?" he slurred. "Why did you wake me up?"

"You weren't asleep, John. Nobody falls asleep in thirty seconds."

John stared at her, this time not bothering to seem anything but fully alert.

"Of course I was asleep," he lied. "I have early appointments tomorrow. Why are you determined to keep me up?"

"I want to know why you're ignoring me. You haven't said a single word to me since you got home."

"What do you want me to say?" John asked and Kate felt her face grow hot with anger. It irritated the shit out of her that instead of admitting that he wasn't speaking to her, he put the burden of his attentiveness onto her. It was grossly unfair and he did it all the time. Kate couldn't help but play into it though.

"Anything," she answered. "You could say anything."

"Tell me what you want me to say and I'll say it."

Kate closed her eyes and prayed for patience. "That's now how it works. You have to engage on your own. I can't tell you what to say. If I did that I'd just be having a conversation with myself."

"Then I don't know what you want me to do. If I don't have any-thing to say and you don't start the conversation, there's nothing to talk about."

"You could try being nice," Kate suggested in a tone that was peril-ously closed to sarcasm.

"I'm always nice."

"No, you're not," Kate protested. "You might think you're being nice but nothing isn't nice."

"I don't even know what that means," John said then turned away, effectively dismissing her.

Kate wanted to smack him. Every time he didn't like the direction of the conversation he'd shut it down and sabotage any opportunity to work through an issue. She wasn't about to let him off the hook. Unfortunately for her, John's wall was up and no amount of talking, shouting, or even setting the bed on fire would rouse him to continue.

Too furious to sleep, Kate got up. In a last dig at her asshole hus-band, she left the lights on when she closed the door behind her. He could drag his fully awake ass up and turn them off himself.

Down in the family room, Kate pulled a book off the shelf and tried to read but she was too angry to make out the words on the page. Instead she stared at the wall in front of her and let her hurt and humiliation consume her.

THREE

Kate awoke to the sound of cabinet doors slamming shut. She opened her eyes against the sun blaring in through the large family room windows and looked over at the kitchen to see John muttering to himself as he got his morning coffee ready.

"I see someone finally decided to get up," he snapped. "I had to get my own shirt this morning."

Clearly, Kate thought. She was surprised to see it was perfectly ironed but unsurprised that he had paired a pale blue shirt with an old black and red patterned tie she was sure she'd tossed into the donation bag.

Rather than play his reindeer games, Kate got up and slowly made her way upstairs to her bathroom. Locking the door behind her, she turned on the shower, undressed and got in. She was still so tired that she didn't know if John tried to enter the bathroom or not. When she turned the water off and got out, the house sounded empty which was a blessing.

She wrapped a towel around herself and left the bathroom to cross to the front windows that looked out onto the driveway. John's car was gone and, with relief, Kate released the breath she didn't realize she was holding.

At least she'd be able to get the girls off to school in peace.

Later that morning with the house to herself, Kate went online to look through her emails again. There was little there and nothing from Bethie for John. Out of curiosity she pulled up Facebook and scrolled through posts from friends and neighbors announcing their love for their significant others and publicly wishing each other happy birthday-anniversary- first date-look at the great and awesome thing my husband-wife-love of my life just did. It was demoralizing to see everyone so damn happy when the only thing John was likely to post would be a photo of the water spots on his grill tagging Kate as the culprit. Kate decided to make things worse for herself and pulled up the list of John's friends and scanned through it until she found a Bethany Stephens. Kate clicked on the name and Bethany's full Facebook page popped up without any bids to send her a friend request to look at her page. Kate shook her head at the lack of security then scrolled through the posts. There were a few posts but there were tons of photos. Almost all of them were selfies of an attractive twenty-something wearing very little and posing provocatively. Many were taken in front of a mirror in a bathroom of questionable cleanliness. Kate was surprised to see only solo pictures. She figured girls like Bethany had tons of friends who spent the majority of their take taking pictures of themselves and each other.

Kate stared at the lovely young girl then, disgusted with herself for Facebook stalking, closed her laptop with a firm snap. Determined to not let her imagination get the best of her, she put on her running shoes and keys then set off for the park.

By that evening, Kate had managed to tire herself out to the point where when the girls asked for breakfast for dinner, she was more than happy to oblige. Unfortunately, John came home early again and looked at their repast of bacon and pancakes with disdain. Kate offered to make him something else but her offer was waved off as John kissed the girls then went into his office and closed the door.

She gave the girls a smile that she didn't really feel then shooed them upstairs for their baths while she cleaned up after their dinner.

Once they were in bed, Kate collapsed on the couch then turned on the television. She was watching the news on CNN when John walked in and sat down at the other end of the couch. A report about the Taliban burning down a school had come on. Kate was surprised to hear John remark on it. She didn't think he was even paying attention.

"That is the problem with you people," he snapped. "You think you can do whatever you want because God told you to. That God is going to just hand you everything you want. So while you're sitting around living some ass backwards life waiting for Him to tell you what to do, nothing happens because He doesn't actually exist. Only idiots would think there's a higher being watching all the moronic shit you do."

Kate turned and stared at him in shock, her face beginning to burn with a sudden anger. She knew it was useless to argue with him but she couldn't just let his comment stand. Silence implied assent and his words, his gross generalizations were unacceptable. She spoke carefully so as not to sound confrontational.

"First, I don't appreciate you including me in your 'you people' rant. Episcopalians don't burn down schools. And second, they aren't burning down schools because of their faith. They're doing it because of their hate. Murder is wrong in Islam as much as it is in Christianity. They're choosing to misinterpret God's will to justify their hatred."

"Maybe you should pray for them," John sneered.

"You should try praying some time. God would be so surprised to hear from you He just might answer," Kate responded with disgust.

To his credit John chuckled but Kate could see resentment behind his eyes. She felt he begrudged her her intelligence. It annoyed him that she didn't just sit and listen to his moralizing like a good little wife.

John smirked at the television as if he already knew what they were going to report. Kate wanted to pursue the insult further then wondered why she bothered. John didn't actually listen when she spoke. He more waited until she stopped so he could tell her why she was wrong. She decided to take away his power and not say anything that he could use against her. From the side eye he was giving her, she could tell he wanted to engage and it made her angry then deeply depressed. Their first actual conversation in days and all he wanted to do was throw verbal knives at her. She stared at the TV in silence then as another story about religious extremists came on, Kate decided to save her sanity and leave the room before he could resume his insults.

Up in her tiny little sanctuary she ironically called her "office" Kate settled into the armchair in the corner and pulled out a book. It was Muriel Barbery's *The Elegance of the Hedgehog* and so far it had served Kate well for its immersive quality. She could escape into the story and let herself be transported far away from the frustrations of her struggling marriage. It had the added benefit of giving her somewhere to go, even if it was just in her head, until John went to bed. She chided herself for her avoidance but with no real issue to resolve and John's penchant for hurling insults, there was no reason to stay in the line of fire.

Warm in her chair with the howling wind dashing all hope for an early spring, Kate listened to the house settle down into silence then began to read.

FOUR

February turned into March and snow turned to rain. Kate felt the cold all the way to her bones and swore that when it was 1000 degrees with a bazillion percent humidity she would not complain. John approached the weather with surprising equanimity. Where everyone else shivered from the damp, he seemed oddly unaffected by it. Kate held out hope that his ridiculously long PMS cycle was finally coming to an end and just in time for them to attempt a social outing.

They had been invited to an anniversary party. Kate didn't know the families in that section of the neighborhood well but the celebrating couple were active at the school and had a son in Emma's class. John was insistent that they go so Kate relented and asked Annabelle, the teenager across the street, to babysit.

When the night of the party arrived, Kate found herself looking forward to it. The winter had been rough with neighbors holing up in their homes for warmth only venturing out to shovel driveways and sidewalks. Kate took care getting dressed and pretended John was taking her out on a date instead of just showing up at a neighbor party. He seemed in relatively good spirits as well though he had very little to say as they drove the short distance to the party. As they walked in, Kate was happy to see several familiar families there and made her way around the rooms catching up with neighbors she hadn't seen in a while. She was so caught up in conversation with several of the school moms that she had completely lost track of time. Kate checked the clock on the stove and realized it was getting late. Annabelle would need to leave soon. She made her excuses to the group surrounding her then went in search of John.

She found him in the dining room in deep but slurring conversation with the couple seated next to him. He was clearly drunk. So drunk that he didn't seem to notice that a woman named Keri, the ex-wife of one of his poker buddies who lived down the street, was sitting on his lap.

Kate cleared her throat then waited for them to realize she was standing there. When they finally looked up she held out her hand.

"I need the keys. Annabelle needs to leave."

John shoved his hand under Keri's ass and slowly pulled the keys out of his pocket. Kate snatched the keys out of his hand.

She didn't wait to see him detach himself from his new friend. Instead she turned and walked out of the house and assumed that he would either follow or find his own way home. She was only mildly surprised to hear him stumble out of the house behind her.

"You could at least wait," he grumbled. Kate ignored him and got into the car.

John fumbled with the car door handle then managed to open it and fall into the seat. He'd barely closed the door behind him when Kate drove away. John cursed her haste but in his drunkenness was barely understandable.

"Did they run out of chairs?" Kate asked.

"What are you talking about?" John mumbled.

"Keri was sitting on your lap."

"No she wasn't."

"Yes she was."

"I don't know what you're talking about."

It was John's go-to defense. Whenever Kate confronted him about anything, he denied it outright like it never happened then tried to turn it around on Kate by implying that she was crazy, or making it up, or whatever the insult du jour was. It was pointless to argue with him. He would rather let it escalate into a massive fight than admit that she was right or that he had done anything wrong.

Kate pulled into their driveway then got out of the car leaving John to figure out things for himself. She could hear his muttered curses behind her as he tried to climb out of his seat. She knew she should help him but unlocked the door and went into the house instead. By the time John made it inside, Kate had thanked Annabelle and paid her. Ignoring her husband, Kate saw the girl to the door and watched her cross the street to make sure she made it home safely.

John still stood swaying in the hallway when Kate closed the door then went up to bed leaving him behind.

The next morning dawned cold both outside and inside the house. Kate awoke to John's cursing as he stumbled around the bedroom trying to get undressed. She had fallen asleep quickly and had remained asleep. John must have slept on the couch.

"I can't believe you left me down there," he snapped as soon as he realized she was awake. "I have appointments this morning."

Kate got up and went into the bathroom without saying a word. She was tired of her husband making his issues, his mistakes her fault.

"You know my cases are down and my reimbursements are down," he said behind her. Of course he had followed her in. Kate finished brushing her teeth then turned to leave but he was blocking the door.

"I can't afford to take a morning off like you can," he continued. "I actually have shit to do without you making things worse. If you could fucking help once in a while things wouldn't be such shit."

"How are your cases and reimbursements being down my fault?" she asked then chided herself for playing into his hands.

"You think this is easy for me?" he asked. It was a non-answer and a question Kate knew better than to respond to. "I work my ass off trying to keep a roof over your heads and food on the table," he continued. "You think you could pull your weight and help me but no."

"You can't keep throwing me into this hole, John," Kate said, her voice cracking. "It's not fair." It was the closest she'd come to expressing how she really felt and of course he chose to dismiss her.

"I'm not doing anything to you," John replied. "You do it to yourself. You think you have it rough here? You don't work. You barely keep the house clean. I have to remind you to get up off your ass and make dinner. What do you do all day anyway?"

"How can you say that?" Kate was incredulous. "I do everything here. I clean, I take care of the girls. And whether you believe it or not there is dinner on the table every single night. And I offered to go back to work when Lizzie started preschool."

"Doing what?" John snorted, "Counseling losers? You couldn't make enough to pay for daycare."

Kate bit her lip to keep from responding. They had had this argument many times before and it always turned out the same in the end. John was pissed and would stay pissed because Kate wasn't doing enough. She knew that in his mind, she could never do enough. Somewhere at some point, Kate had ceased to have any value to her husband. To him she was an expense, like an employee and an underperforming one at that. All those neighbors who posted about the love and appreciation they had for their spouses were completely alien to her. Kate wanted to call it all bullshit but the reality was it was her marriage that was bullshit. She felt a worm of pain rising up from the pit of her stomach to wrap itself around her heart. Then it squeezed and Kate knew if she didn't leave the room soon, her unsympathetic husband would bear witness to the grief that was squeezing the life out of her.

She turned to leave only to hear John call out, "I need a shirt."

Of course you do, she thought then went into the closet.

Tears streamed from her eyes as she ironed the wrinkles out of the shirt in front of her. She could barely see and knew tears had fallen onto the cotton. She dragged the iron over them, sealing her sorrow into the fabric.

Kate pulled the crisp shirt off the ironing board and carried it into the bathroom to hand it to John.

"You're welcome," she muttered then turned to leave.

"I shouldn't have to thank you," John argued. He didn't even notice, or care, that his wife was crying. Instead he inhaled in a verbal wind up to hurl more recriminations at her. Kate didn't want to hear it and closed the door on his next words. Instead of going down into the kitchen to make his coffee, Kate went into her office and closed the door. With any luck the girls would stay asleep until he left giving her time to force back the tears that still fell.

By the end of that day, Kate was dead inside. She tried to smile for the girls but the truth was she had no joy left in her. Shit rolled downhill in her world and she tried hard to stop it before it affected Emma and Lizzie. They were old enough to know something was wrong but too young to know what was making their mother so sad. Kate did her best but her best was subdued if not despondent.

She found she was losing time while she went through the motions of her day-to-day life. As March turned into April, the dullness had permeated every cell of her being until nothing John said or did really mattered. When he could no longer get a reaction from her, he simply stopped talking. It was both a relief and a curse because it kept Kate apart. His silence wasn't hateful or punishing. It was like she simply ceased to exist for him. If he did say something to her, it was cold and dispassionate. If she responded he reacted with surprise as if they had just met and didn't realize she wasn't a deaf mute.

By mid-April though, John's antagonism was coming back around full circle. Kate had managed to stay out of his way but unless she left the house completely, John still managed to find her.

"You know, whatever this thing you're going through is, you'd better get a handle on it. You're too depressing to be around and it's going to affect the girls."

Kate ignored the comment. She knew she needed to get it together. John was the majority of her problem but talking to him was useless and she knew he'd never agree to go to marriage counseling. The fact that she herself was a counselor who couldn't communicate with her own husband was a sore point with her and she knew any conversation she tried to bring up would be met with disdain if not outright rejected.

She told herself that with the weather changing, so would her melancholy. The rain had finally stopped and the sun shown as if the season had officially decided to stay. Leaves were starting to come back and though the air was still crisp, the first buds bloomed giving the promise of a lovely spring.

John continued to nag but Kate had had a whole month to build a wall against his criticisms and could weather them without feeling provoked. When he couldn't get a reaction out of her, John gave up and left her alone.

Kate found her depression easing and she was enjoying herself more whenever it was just her and her daughters. Emma seemed relieved that her mother was almost back to normal though Lizzie had been mostly unaware during the whole horrible ordeal. John's late nights resumed and he'd even taken a couple of weekends to travel for continuing education conferences. Kate hated to admit it but she loved it when he went away. It didn't happen often but when it did it was like a bad smell had left the house.

Kate took advantage of his absence to give the house a thorough cleaning and cull through the tons of toys and clothes to pull out whatever she and the girls no longer needed or no longer fit. By the end of one weekend, she had several large trash bags filled with donations. As an afterthought, she threw in John's old ratty black and red tie then tied them all shut and drove them to the local donation center.

By the time John returned from his trip, the house was thoroughly uncluttered and sparkling. As a reward for getting rid of so many of their toys, Kate took Emma and Lizzie to the store to shop for swim suits. The neighborhood pool would be opening at the end of the month and in their house at least, it was a really big deal.

When the big day arrived, Kate went up to get Emma and Lizzie ready for their day. They were especially excited to be one of the first to jump in the new pool. With their new suits on, new beach towels and plenty of snacks in hand, Kate and the girls made their way down the street. Kate loved that the pool and playground were so close to her house. It only took a short five minute walk for them while other families had to drive and hope for parking.

As they arrived, Kate was happy to see a handful of families she knew already waiting. Emma and Lizzie joined their friends at the gate while Kate waited at the back of the group giving a polite smile when one was warranted.

The morning had been a tornado of criticisms from John about their plan to "waste a whole day" at the pool even though it was a holiday weekend. Kate was glad he declined Emma's plea to come with them and was grateful that he was at least civil to his daughter. As she waited with the others, she felt numbness come over her that she hadn't felt in a while. She knew her depression was settling in again and welcomed it over the grief she'd felt previously. She hoped that John's cycle of anger would move into his usual zone of silence. Their relationship no long ventured into good but it was at least tolerable when he was just ignoring her.

Finally the young people who had been hired to guard and run the pool all stepped out and assumed their places up in the chairs. Kate was happy to see their babysitter, Annabelle opening the gate. A line formed as patrons handed in their ID cards then scrambled to find the best seat. With so many little kids in line, all the tables and chairs around the kidney shaped shallow pool were taken in no time so Kate made her way to the other side and took a table in the corner near the deep end of the big pool. Both her girls could swim well so she didn't worry that they would need much assistance in the water.

It was quieter in the corner with its distance from the large mushroom fountain that rained freezing water on little bodies in the smaller pool and Kate had chosen the corner opposite the small fenced-in baby pool in the corner. She pulled her book out of her bag and started to read keeping one eye on her girls. When it was obvious that Emma and Lizzie were in good hands with the many lifeguards around, Kate let herself fall asleep.

The next morning, the girls were up and ready early for another day at the pool. John again tried to argue against their going but relented when he saw how much Emma and Lizzie were looking forward to it. Kate was fuming though. It made her so angry that he would take out his anger towards her on the girls, even indirectly. It was like he begrudged her any small bit of fun or happiness. Why was he so determined she be miserable? He was going off to play golf for the day. It wasn't like he needed her home to wait on him.

She was still chewing over John's attitude when she stepped inside the gate at the pool. She was surprised to see an extraordinarily handsome young man working the front table and wondered why on earth someone who looked like that would work at a pool. She was so caught up in her musings she didn't realize she'd handed him her pass.

"Thank you, Mrs. Richardson. You can get your pass back on your way out."

He smiled. Kate felt the blood rush to her face. She nodded dumbly and moved aside to let the family behind her drop off their pool passes.

Thankfully, her neighbor and good friend Michelle was waving her over from the other side of the pool. Kate hurried over and claimed the pool chaise next to her.

"What do you think of our aquatic Adonis?" Michelle quipped with less sarcasm than usual.

"Uh, yeah, he's a cutie all right," she answered in what she hoped was a steady voice.

"Our Patrick has surpassed cuteness," Michelle said through her yawn, then rolled over to even out the tan on her back. "He's damn near perfection."

Kate couldn't agree more. Luckily she was spared any further conversation when Michelle promptly fell asleep. Kate was thankful she had sunglasses on. From her vantage point, she could watch him go about the business of running the pool without being obvious.

He really was perfection, though she couldn't put her finger on what made him so, when the entire pool staff was made up of nubile young men. On the surface, Patrick seemed like the best example of any young man his age. Tall and thin with a tan so dark, he appeared molded out of caramel. His dark hair was cut short and otherwise left to its perfectly windblown self.

Kate was studying him so intently that she didn't realize he was looking straight at her until he flashed her a dazzling smile. Blushing furiously, she smiled back and turned away in search of a book, towel, or anything to hide behind. In desperation, she pulled an old *Rolling Stone* from her pool bag and immersed herself in the pages of a year-old article about climate change.

Michelle woke up over an hour later.

"Good grief, how long have I been asleep?" she asked, bleary-eyed.

Kate checked the clock conveniently located next to the pool office. "Since ten."

"I've got to go pick Kelly up from camp." Michelle groaned as she pulled on her cover-up. "Are you guys going to stay?"

"No. We'll go with you. I didn't bring anything for lunch."

She felt ridiculously self-conscious as she gathered her girls then followed Michelle to pick up their passes. She'd been caught staring at the overly handsome pool boy and was still horribly embarrassed.

She was grateful to have Michelle to hide behind and trusted that her friend would take her pass (and with more aplomb than Kate could ever hope to muster). She moved to follow Michelle out of the gate when she heard her name.

"Mrs. Richardson?"

Kate turned back to see Patrick smiling at her. "You forgot your pass."

Kate walked back and took it from him, her fingers burning from where they brushed against his.

"Sorry," she mumbled, embarrassed beyond belief.

"No problem. See you tomorrow," he answered then gave her a dazzling smile. Kate wanted to stare again but ducked her head and turned away.

Later that night, Kate sat and watched her husband complain about his dried out, overcooked dinner that she and the girls had enjoyed hours earlier. He had strolled in late, reeking of alcohol and ready to complain about the lack of fresh food on the table. She couldn't help but recall the sunny smile the pool manager had given her.

As divine as their neighborhood pool manager was, by contrast, the man she had pledged her life to was as far removed from the lovely pool boy as a man could be. Where Patrick was tan and fit, John had let himself go, and his slightly pudgy body was a pale, mottled pink, not unlike the underbelly of a dead fish. And instead of Patrick's calm self-assurance, John fidgeted about the house in an endless search for slights and shortcomings in everyone around him. Kate knew this part of his funk was a phase, happening in direct correlation with the periodic decline in his business. Whoever said dentists were rich didn't know any dentists personally. Between the reduction in insurance reimbursements and the improvement in overall dental health, John's practice was struggling. She was tired of his making her the scapegoat though. Their marriage traveled in a circle of anger to nothing then back to anger. Love and joy never made an appearance anymore. Kate had hoped the winter had been a big part of his anger towards her but even with the change in season he still treated her like she was an inconvenience.

Since his hours were long and erratic again, it had fallen to Kate to take care of their girls, the house, and everything else in their lives that wasn't related to dentistry. John was now regularly coming home at odd hours, usually missing dinner and even the girls' bedtime. Kate often wondered how much she and the girls were really on his radar. *Not much*, she figured. She couldn't remember the last time she and John had gone to bed together, let alone had sex.

When Michelle called to schedule another poolside tanning session, Kate found herself taking more care with her appearance, even going so far as to coordinate her jewelry with the color of her swimsuit. She knew she was being an idiot, but when she got to the pool, she noticed she wasn't the only one. An abundance of new swimsuits (and in some cases, fully made-up faces) dotted the pool deck. She clearly wasn't the only one smitten with the new pool manager.

Kate searched her pool bag and dug up the darkest sunglasses she could find, so that no one could tell she was staring at him from across the pool. Her eyes followed him whenever he filled in on the guard stand or checked the chemical content of the water. Every so often, he would jump in and cross the length of the pool in long, swift strokes that cut the water like butter then climb out, water sluicing across the tan flesh of his body.

She was so caught up in watching him that she failed to realize that he was walking over to where she and Michelle were sitting.

"Hey," he called out then sat at the end of the empty lounge chair next to her. Michelle rolled over and stared at him, her eyebrows up. "Aren't you hot over here? You've been sitting in the sun this whole time."

Kate gave him an awkward smile. "Starting to. I'd get in but I hate getting splashed."

Patrick gave her his dazzling smile. "I know what you mean. Those kids are pretty crazy. You want me to have them call an adult swim?"

Kate was about to demur when Michelle spoke up. "Heck yeah. Get those kids out of there so we can get in."

Patrick laughed then got up and walked over to the guard stand. A minute later whistles blew for adult swim and a groaning mass of children exited the pool.

"Come on," Michelle urged. "Let's get in before they lynch us."

FIVE

The next day Emma and Lizzie were ready to go even before the pool opened.

"I hope Patrick can play with us today," Kate heard Emma say to her sister. It made Kate a little sad. They should want to play with their dad but John had yet to spend any time with them at home, let alone take them to the pool.

Michelle and her brood met them at the end of the driveway and they walked the rest of the way to the pool en masse.

Emma and Lizzie were disappointed to see that Patrick wasn't there. If Kate were honest with herself, she'd admit that she too was a little disappointed. Patrick had a way of pulling her out of her own head. The pool had turned into her emotional safe place, mostly because John never ventured there. Kate knew it was ridiculous but she felt calm as soon as she walked in the gates, as if the space inside the fence was her own private sanctuary, albeit one where everyone in the neighborhood was invited.

Kate and Michelle took a table in the far corner then settled into the lounge chairs nearby. Kate pulled out a book and Michelle helped her youngest build a lounge chair towel fort to play in until the older girls realized what he had and appropriated it for their own use.

It wasn't long until both Kate and Michelle were dozing in their chairs.

Kate felt a cold drip falling on her face and opened her eyes to see Lizzie leaning over her, her sweet face blocking the sun.

"We're hungry," she announced and Kate wasn't surprised. Next to baby dolls, Lizzie's favorite thing to do was eat.

Kate sat up and pulled her pool bag over. "Ok. I think I have some snacks in here."

Lizzie shook her head. "I don't want snacks."

Kate looked at her watch and was surprised to see it was almost lunchtime. She reached over and gently shook Michelle who sat up blinking.

"You want me to go get the kids some hot dogs?" she offered.

Michelle nodded. "I'll do lunch tomorrow then."

Kate turned to search for her pool cover and flip flops when Lizzie shouted next to her.

"Patrick!"

Kate turned to see Patrick striding over, his arms filled with bags.

"I wasn't sure if you guys had eaten lunch yet but I got everyone something."

Lizzie was hopping up and down as Patrick set the bags down on the table.

"They opened a new Mission BBQ near here so I thought everyone might like some sandwiches and mac and cheese."

Kate had heard of Mission BBQ and had heard the food was great. John frequented the one near his Canton office but had never taken her there.

Like the Pied Piper, Patrick soon had a crowd of children around him, Lizzie still hopping up and down like an excited terrier. To their credit, they all waited patiently as Patrick pulled containers out of the bags.

Kate turned to Michelle who was regarding Patrick with a weird look.

"We should offer to pay," Kate whispered, interrupting her reverie.

Michelle nodded then grabbed her wallet from her pool bag. Kate did likewise and handed Michelle a twenty dollar bill, unofficially appointing her their financial emissary.

Michelle smirked at Kate but stood and went over to help Patrick.

"Here, hon," she said, handing him the cash. "We can't let you pay for all these kids."

Patrick shook his head. "I've got this. I wouldn't have done it if I wasn't willing to pay," he answered. "Who wants mac and cheese?" Hands went up around him. As Patrick started handing out containers, Michelle slipped the money into his pocket then gave Kate a smirk. Kate chuckled then made her face blank as Patrick handed her a container.

"I got you the brisket and some potato salad," he said. "I don't know what they put in the potato salad but it is kick ass."

Kate accepted a fork and tasted the savory blocks of warm potatoes. Patrick was right, it was delicious. She accepted a dollop of barbecue sauce from Michelle and tasted the beef letting out a moan of appreciation. It was as good as the potatoes, better even. Kate understood why John raved about it so much. She felt a small twinge of resentment that he'd kept it to himself then set it aside. John was like a cat with a food bowl and her hurt feelings weren't going to change that.

When they were done, Kate helped clean everyone up then sent them off to the shallow pool to cool off and digest before swimming again. Patrick had been chatting with Michelle then got up to start his shift.

"That was really nice of him, wasn't it?" Kate asked when she returned from throwing away their trash.

Michelle made a weird a face and nodded. "Yeah, that was above and beyond. Not that I'm complaining. He just better realize that those kids are going to expect that all the time."

Kate nodded then sat back on her lounge chair.

Why had Patrick brought them food? It was certainly unusual given the fact that the pool was filled with other families and he hadn't brought anything for them. Kate watched him go about the business of running the pool then realized he was smiling at her. She blushed and turned to face the book in her lap. What the heck was going on?

Kate stared at the words on the page in front of her and let her mind wander.

On Patrick's days off, Kate sat on the steps leading into the shallow end to watch her girls play. Even though they were young, both girls had taken summer swim lessons in previous years. They were good swimmers and rarely needed help in the water. Her younger daughter, Lizzie, was not quite six but could navigate the depths like a fearless young seal.

It was during one of his absences that Kate ventured to the side of the pool to soak her feet while Michelle sat in the shallow end with her youngest. They were idly chatting when Kate felt someone sit down beside her.

She glanced over, assuming it was another mom, then almost choked to see Patrick smiling at her.

"Too hot for the chairs, isn't it?"

Kate smiled and glanced at Michelle, who raised her eyebrows and swished her son through the water.

"Where are the girls?" he asked. Kate was about to answer when Lizzie swam over and ran up the steps to climb onto Patrick.

"Throw me in! Throw me in!" she ordered, in the way only adorable five-year-olds can.

Patrick laughed and carried Lizzie into the deeper part of the pool, where he spent the next half-hour throwing her into the air, her little body spinning before it hit the water. Not to be outdone, Kate's older daughter, Emma, swam over and joined the fun. Kate watched as Patrick let the girls jump off of him, something their father would never have done.

Soon, it was time for him to actually work, so Patrick carried her protesting girls over and dropped them near Kate.

"Sorry ladies, but I don't get paid to play," he joked as he lifted himself onto the concrete next to Kate. He leaned into her and whispered something that Kate couldn't even begin to hear over the blood roaring in her ears.

She was both relieved and heartbroken when he stood up to leave. She forced herself to look at her girls and not watch him cross the concrete.

Michelle *was* watching him, however, as she moved to sit on the steps by Kate's feet.

"I think someone's got a little crush on you," she said.

Kate snorted and shook her head. "He's just being nice to the girls."

"Uh huh," Michelle answered, but left it at that.

Kate didn't think Patrick had a crush on her but he did start spending a lot of time with them over the next couple of weeks. Once she recovered from her initial shock of having such a beautiful man sitting next to her, Kate found Patrick remarkably easy to talk to. He was older than she'd previously thought and was working towards his master's degree in public health. With her background in social work, they had a lot to talk about and Kate found him intelligent and personable.

The girls definitely benefitted from his attention. They took full advantage of Patrick's presence and had no problems convincing him to come into the water to play with them. She was grateful he was so kind and patient with them and she could see the joy on their faces whenever he singled them out amongst the crowd of children at the pool. When he wasn't there, they were sad until Annabelle, who had just come off her lifeguard shift, stepped in to take his place.

Kate felt gratified that her girls had other adults and young people around to make them feel loved. There was so little at home lately that she would take anything she could get.

SIX

She knew something was wrong the minute she opened the door. It was as if the very air was tainted with whatever bad news waited for her inside. Kate closed the door behind her and listened. She could hear the clock on the mantle ticking and the muffled sounds of children playing outside...and something else. Kate walked through the foyer and around the corner to the kitchen. The something else was John, home five hours early and sitting at the breakfast table. Kate stopped short. From the tension in his face, she knew something terrible was about to be said and her mind ran through all the possible scenarios. He's lost his job (even though he was a dentist. Did dentists lose their jobs?), or someone has died, or there's been an accident, or his mother is sick, or he's sick, or someone has cancer.

John started to make small talk, but Kate interrupted him. "Just say it. Whatever it is, just say it."

John sighed then rubbed his face. "Maybe you should sit down first."

Kate shook her head. "No, John. Rip the band-aid off fast and just say it."

For a split second, Kate saw a look of irritation cross his face.

"It's Bethany. She's pregnant."

Kate just stood there, her brain fighting to process what she'd just heard. Bethany who worked for John in his dental practice? She couldn't think of anything less relevant.

"So?"

John looked away, his expression embarrassed. "*I* got her pregnant," he said to the wall, his tone oddly defensive.

Kate felt the tips of her fingers go numb, so much she couldn't tell how fiercely she gripped the side of the counter top. . Her teeth were clenched so tightly she could hardly speak. "Let me get this straight. You're telling me that you fucked dental hygienist Barbie and knocked her up? You are one stupid piece of shit."

John's expression of surprise might have been funny under any other circumstance, but at that moment, it made Kate even angrier. She wanted to march over and slap it right off his face, but the idea of touching anything on him after Bethany did repulsed her.

Instead, she stood her ground. "So, I suppose you intend to make an honest woman of her?"

John looked uncomfortable. "Well...no. I hadn't thought that far ahead. I was hoping we could work this out."

Kate was incredulous. "You've got to be kidding me. Work *what* out? You had sex with your employee and got her pregnant. You're not going to be able to fix this one."

"The pregnancy was an accident," John tried to explain, but Kate wouldn't hear it.

"This isn't an accident. It's not like Bethany fell on your dick and somehow ended up pregnant. You made a choice. You made a choice to fuck a woman who wasn't your wife and you made a choice to not wear a condom, and since it's highly unlikely she got pregnant the first time you fucked her, you made a choice to do it often enough to knock her up." Kate crossed her arms and glared at him. "Unfortunately for you, you have run out of choices."

John had the nerve to look angry. "So what are you implying?"

Kate was so enraged she wanted to grab a knife and stab him in the head. "I'm not implying anything. I'm telling you. You want to play happy family with your office slut, go right ahead."

"Uh, I wasn't planning on leaving," John tried to sneer but fell short.

Kate's look was deadly. "Oh no, my friend. Whatever you were planning is irrelevant. You *are* leaving. Right now."

John stared at her, his expression stubborn. "No."

Kate's eyes narrowed. "You don't want to push me on this one, John. I am practically homicidal at this moment."

A variety of expressions crossed John's face as he struggled with the desire to stay and fight it out, battling the reality that he'd lost the moment he'd opened his mouth.

Kate didn't move as he stalked past her and down the basement stairs. She didn't move as he pulled a suitcase out of the closet under the basement steps, slamming the door, and dragged it up to their bedroom. She didn't even flinch as she listened to drawers opening then slamming closed and the hangers in the closet shifting. She hardly blinked as she heard the heavy thump of the suitcase on the floor at the bottom of the stairs. She didn't turn at the long moment of silence as John looked at her for whatever reason she could not possibly conceive of. It wasn't until the front door slammed behind him that she finally took a breath.

Kate picked up the phone and called Michelle. Kelly answered with, "Aw, do they have to come home now?"

"No," Kate answered curtly. "Please let me talk to your mom." She listened as Kelly and her girls cheered, then the clatter of the phone being handed over to Michelle.

"What's up?" Michelle asked, her radar obviously up with the squealing human alarms behind her.

Kate tried to keep her voice steady. "John's hygienist is pregnant. He's gone. Can the girls stay with you tonight?"

She was grateful that Michelle got it right away, without any need for explanation.

"Absolutely. Do you want me to come over? I have wine." Michelle offered without preamble.

"Definitely tomorrow." Kate knew that Michelle would not need anything more than that and hung up knowing her friend would know exactly what she needed.

The house was as empty as Kate felt. Without direction, she wandered up to the small bedroom she'd turned into her own little sitting room. There she felt cocooned by all the things she'd bought over the years that John had either criticized or downright forbidden from the family rooms. She stared out the windows that, as it happened, faced the pool, but for the first time in weeks, she hardly noticed it.

SEVEN

John's departure from their lives was abrupt yet only marginally upsetting to his daughters. He'd been around so rarely that they hardly missed him, and at the end, when he was home, his demeanor toward Kate had been equal parts harsh and dismissive to the point that the silence following his exit was actually a blessing for all of them. It was like a cloud of poison gas...or an especially vile fart had dissipated, leaving them gratefully gasping for the clean air of freedom.

It also didn't hurt that they were truly children of their generation, where parents divorced then remarried with families blending on a regular basis. For Kate, all that was left was the actual divorce proceedings. Even though she could sue on the grounds of adultery, John had humbled himself enough to ask her to spare his nonexistent reputation so she agreed to a traditional separation.

The girls were still in school when John moved out. Kate had hoped that he would at least have some kind of conversation with them himself but he'd thrown his last grenade as he carried the last of his clothes out.

"It doesn't matter what I say to them," he answered in response to her pleas. "You're going to make me out to be the bad guy anyway."

It wasn't true and it hurt her that he would say that. Even at the end of everything, he still couldn't help but tear her down. Kate didn't have it in her to remind him that they were old enough to decide for themselves if he was a bad guy or not. She didn't need to turn her children against their father. He'd done a great job of that all on his own.

She let him have the last word and stood just inside the doorway to watch him drive away.

Later that evening when it was the time John would normally come home, Kate wasn't surprised that neither Emma nor Lizzie asked about their father. If they noticed there wasn't a place set for him at the table, they didn't say anything and they went to bed as if nothing had really changed. And in a way, it hadn't. John had been away more than he had been home and when he did come home it was well after they had gone to bed. At the time it bothered her but now she saw it as a mixed blessing. They couldn't miss what they didn't know.

For her though, she still had to deal with the drama of her divorce. Now that he was out of the house and living with his mistress, John's attitude improved and with it his ability to communicate with Kate in a civil manner. Since she'd agreed to avoid citing adultery, Kate filed for divorce based on irreconcilable differences instead. Her attorney didn't like this but admitted it gave them leverage everywhere else. Ironically, it was Bethany who admitted to the court that she was pregnant so John had no choice but to accept his own adultery as grounds for the divorce. Kate suspected the admission was deliberate so that John would be free sooner. In Maryland it meant an immediate divorce without the year-long mandatory separation. They were done.

Even though she was entitled to spousal and child support, the financial aspect of the divorce settlement was going to take longer. John still begrudged her any form of support and Kate knew she needed to go back to work, even if it was only on a part-time basis. Though John's leaving was still fresh and his attitude was still amicable, Kate knew it was only a matter of time before the petty side of his nature re-exerted itself, and she wanted to be ready.

Despite the terrible economy, there were a surprising number of positions for social workers in Maryland. With a little bit of foot work and a lot of luck, Kate had two solid offers in front of her. Only a couple of weeks after her separation, she was happy to accept a position as a counselor at a special needs school. The position didn't officially start until the fall so she still had most of the summer free to work around her girls' schedules of playdates and half-day camps. By the time they started school, she would start work and be able to earn enough to keep them comfortable as long as John didn't renege on his initial financial agreement. Kate had no idea what his life was like now, but she knew him well enough to know that, at any minute, John could pull the rug out from under them.

Though the dissolution of her marriage was easier than she thought it would be, Kate found her social situation untenable. Since their neighborhood was somewhat isolated from the rest of their small city, people knew each other's business and if they didn't know, they would speculate. And the neighborhood was small enough that everyone was on least a nodding basis with everyone else. It didn't take long for everyone to know that John had moved out and to guess why. Divorce was like a virus that no one wanted to catch but every-one wanted to discuss.

On the surface, the families around her were supportive and her few close friends remained by her side. But like any community of women, there were those who took secret delight in the fact that this time it was someone else going through the gossip ringer. Rumors spread throughout the community and Kate found herself the victim of endless fake smiles and behind-the-hand speculation. It wasn't until Lizzie blurted out at a birthday party that her dad was going to marry his dental assistant, that the rest of their small world learned the truth of her situation.

Kate turned her back on those that did not wish her well and instead found support within the community of her church.

Even though John was nonreligious at best, Kate had wanted her girls to have at least a working knowledge of Christianity, so she enrolled them in preschool at the local Episcopal church. St. John's had an excellent reputation as far as academics went, with the added benefit of a worldly but sympathetic clergy. And despite the large number of young families, there were enough single parents there to make her feel less conspicuous.

She'd started out going regularly but faced with John's increasing disapproval they hadn't been to church in a while. But on their first Sunday back, when they entered the hall for the contemporary service, it was like they never left. Though the historic church held a worship service at the exact same time, Kate thought the contemporary service would be more child-friendly. Since Sunday school didn't start until the fall, Kate figured the girls could withstand an hour's worth of worship with the promise that they could go out for brunch afterward.

As they made their way into the hall, several parishioners greeted them. Annabelle, the girl who lived on their street and had been the girls' longtime babysitter, came up and gave them big hugs and offered to sit with them during worship. Kate had brought activity bags, but having Annabelle nearby to distract them was an added bonus. They found some empty seats near the middle and sat down.

Though she preferred the ambience of the historic church, Kate felt a familiar sense of calm fall over her as the service began. The youth minister led the service and her gentle voice had a storytelling quality that kept the girls entranced. Reverend Jess was a lovely pixie of a woman who was well-suited to the ministry of children and youth. Kate enjoyed the simplicity of her sermon so much she was disappointed when it ended.

Kate and the girls followed the crowd out into the common area for coffee and pastries. At the sight of all those delicious glazed treats, Emma and Lizzie practically pulled off Kate's arm begging for a donut.

"OK," she laughed, "but don't be surprised if you're not hungry later."

Emma and Lizzie smiled happily and got in line. Kate turned to see Reverend Jess at her elbow.

"Hey, Kate," she greeted her with warmth. "I wanted to tell you how happy I am to see you and the girls here today."

"Oh, thanks." Kate was embarrassed. They had been gone for such a long time. "I thought...Well, with everything that's going on, the girls and I needed to reconnect with our church family."

Reverend Jess's expression turned concerned. "And how *are* you doing?"

"The girls are doing well, but I'm not quite there yet," Kate admitted. "I thought coming here could help."

Reverend Jess nodded. "You know, my door is always open if you need to talk it out. And I'd be happy to work with the girls if you find they're having adjustment problems."

Kate smiled. "Thank you."

Reverend Jess looked thoughtful. "You know, the clergy have been trying to put together a support network here at the church. Our community has been growing so much that we're finding a real need for a more organized system for pastoral counseling and support. Would you be interested in helping us?"

Kate was surprised. "Sure, if you think I can help."

"I think with your background and your experience, you could be of great help," Reverend Jess replied. "Sometimes, it's in our service to others where we find hope for ourselves. Let's have lunch this week and talk about it."

Kate was touched at the other woman's gesture. She recognized the Reverend's attempt to give her a sense of purpose, and she was grateful. Kate watched as she moved away to greet other parishioners, then made her own way through the crowd saying hellos and receiving hugs here and there. Halfway across the common, she met Annabelle with two very sticky girls in tow.

"Wow," Annabelle laughed. "You'd think they'd never seen a donut before."

Kate chuckled. "Well, there goes brunch. Thanks for looking after them."

"No problem. I've got to help clean up. I'll see you next week?"

"Sure," Kate answered then took her possession of her sticky but happy girls.

"Are we still going out for breaklunch?" Lizzie asked as they made their way to the bathroom to clean up.

Kate laughed. "Sure," she answered again. She'd love nothing more than to have breaklunch with her precious girls.

EIGHT

Not one to waste time, Reverend Jess phoned a few days later with the news that she had a small group of newly and soon-to-be divorced women who were in need of a facilitator. Kate complimented Reverend Jess's efficiency with a joke then gave her a handful of days that would work. When she hung up, she wondered if it had been wise to agree to help others when she hadn't really worked out all of her own issues yet.

By the end of the week Kate had set her doubts aside and resolved to at least try to help someone else if she couldn't help herself. She knew she needed to cut the ties of her broken marriage and resolved to do it immediately. The first step was to remove John physically from her life. Now that he was out of the house, it fell to Kate to pack up eleven years of his stuff. Though he'd taken some of his clothes the day he moved out, their master bedroom closet was still filled with casual clothes, suits, and seasonal items. John had arranged for movers to come and pick up the rest of his things so Kate dragged boxes upstairs and set about cleaning out all of his clothes. When she was done, she dragged the boxes back downstairs then started on his office. Rather than try to carry finished boxes, Kate carried the books, trophies, and miscellaneous papers out to the garage instead.

Her mind was a million miles away as she stood in the garage taping up the last of John's books. In the absence of any intellectual activity, her mind reeled with the truth of her situation. Despite the fact that the divorce proceedings had been mercifully quick since the custody arrangements were uncontested (and their attorneys were able to work out a preliminary financial settlement), Kate worried that John would still try to punish her. It was the twisted way he usually dealt with problems. She knew in his mind he had been generous considering it was his fault they were splitting up. It was only a matter of time before something went south for him and he needed another scapegoat.

She was just finishing up when she heard a discreet knock on the wooden frame of the garage door. She turned, her fingers tucking errant strands of hair behind her ear. "Yes?" She couldn't imagine why a breathtakingly handsome twenty-something man would be standing in her garage of all places.

He waved. "Hi."

Kate could hardly answer but found her voice after some discreet clearing of her throat. "Hi."

"Um, we haven't seen you at the pool for a while, and we were wondering if everything was all right?"

Kate wondered who the "we" could be but couldn't bring herself to ask. Instead, she shrugged. "I don't...I, um...Everything is..." She shook her head and shrugged again. "I don't really have an answer for that."

Patrick took a step closer. "I'm sorry. I don't want to bother you. I just wanted to make sure you weren't mad at us, I mean, me...or anything."

Kate shook her head and began to speak when Patrick took another step toward her.

"It's just...I heard some of the other ladies at the pool talking and, well, I wasn't trying to eavesdrop or anything, but they were saying that

Mr. Richardson moved out and I really just want to make sure you were OK." Patrick took another step toward her, and Kate felt her heart begin to beat again.

"I'm OK," she answered sincerely, her smile sad. "John left because I told him to. He was having an affair with a girl in his office and got her pregnant. So I told him to leave."

Kate felt her heart pounding as Patrick reached out to take her hand. "I'm really sorry."

"Don't be." She laughed. "It was inevitable. We were done a long time ago."

Patrick continued to look at her, his thumb moving over the tops of her fingers. She could tell he was struggling with something. She opened her mouth to ask what was wrong when he brought his other hand up and gently touched the tips of his fingers to her cheek.

Kate could hardly breathe. She had no idea why he was there or what he wanted from her. All she knew was that he was standing incredibly close. For a split second, she wondered if she'd remembered to brush her teeth. But then he kissed her.

His kiss was as perfect as the rest of him. Warm and strong and gentle, his lips searched hers for the perfect spot. She closed her eyes and drank him in. When he pulled away, she didn't want to open her eyes, afraid that it was all a dream. Instead, she leaned into him and felt his arms go around her as he pulled her close, her head fitting perfectly under his chin.

She could hear his heart pounding in his chest. His voice rumbled as he began to speak.

"Kate?" he ventured, as if trying it out.

"Hmmm?"

"Could I come and see you again?"

With her cheek pressed against his chest, Kate nodded.

Kate finally pulled away, feeling awkward and desperate.

"Thanks for checking up on me," she stammered. "You really didn't have to."

Patrick smiled, and she found she was smiling back.

Later at dinner, Kate picked at her food and relived the feeling of Patrick's arms around her. It had been so long since anyone other than her girls had hugged her that she felt like she was going to explode.

Then reality reasserted itself. She was easily ten years older than he was, if not more. What was she thinking? The last thing she wanted was to be somebody's conquest. Granted it had been a long time since anyone looked at her with anything resembling affection but the pool boy? Really? She was the worst kind of cliché no matter how sweet or handsome Patrick was.

Kate tortured herself for the better part of the next day then resolved to cut it off with Patrick when he came back...if he came back.

That evening Kate left for her first support group meeting at the church. She was surprised to see a car in the lot behind Rose Hill, the large house the church used for meetings and classes. She had thought she would arrive early enough to have a chance to get herself together before the meeting

When she stepped in there was a woman sitting in the room to the left. What had originally been the house's living room was now an open space with chairs arranged in a semi-circle. A table had been set up at one end to hold a coffee maker and snacks. Kate noticed the coffee maker was already running though there were no snacks since she held them in a bag in her hand. The woman jumped up and took the bag from her.

"You must be Kate!" she said with a weird chirping voice. "I'm Linda. I'm one of your members." The woman, Linda, was a good decade older than Kate with a tight hair helmet of curls and wearing an ill-fitting red suit with black tights and white shoes. Linda glanced into the bag and made a face. "What are those? Are they pastries?"

"They're macaroons," Kate replied. She was suddenly incredibly annoyed with this woman and felt terrible about it. She was there to help, not judge, but something about Linda rubbed her the wrong way.

"Oh," Linda made a face then placed the bag down next to the coffee maker. "Well maybe they'll be familiar to the other ladies. I'm assuming someone else is coming, right?" Linda tittered as if she'd made a joke.

Kate gave her a tight smile. "Group doesn't start for another half an hour so I'm sure they are on their way. If you'll excuse me..." she said then left the room before Linda could answer.

Down the hall was a small office next to the kitchen that Reverend Jess had recommended Kate use as a storage space for any materials she would need. On the desk she found a post-it with her name on it stuck to a stack of newsletters and other information pieces. Kate pulled the stack apart and looked through the papers then added her own support materials to the stack. When she heard the front door open, she ventured out to find a stunningly beautiful woman standing just inside and looking around with an amused expression.

"Hi," Kate called out then crossed the hall to the woman. "Are you here for the support group?"

The woman looked at her and was about to respond when Linda stepped out of the doorway.

"Come in come in," she chirped then reached out to grab the other woman's elbow.

"I can walk, thanks," the woman answered in a long southern drawl then turned to Kate. "Are you Kate?" she asked.

"Yes," Kate answered, "I'm Kate your facilitator."

"Thank God," the woman answered with a glance at Linda. "I'm Georgia. There are some others outside who aren't sure where they're supposed to go. You want me to go get them?"

"I'll do it," Linda cried then darted out the door.

"Great," Georgia muttered under her breath. "Maybe she won't come back."

Kate suppressed a chuckle then followed Georgia into the room.

Unfortunately Linda did come back and with three very nervous women with her. Kate stood and introduced herself and was relieved to meet Evelyn who Reverend Jess had warned was a member of one of the church's long-standing families. She'd pictured some noble matriarch but Evelyn was really just a small quiet woman who looked like she needed a hug. Kate led Evelyn to the chair next to her then watched with amusement as Linda negotiated seating so she'd end up next to Georgia.

"So, let's begin. I'd like to welcome you to our first 'Women Facing Divorce' meeting. Since we are new we might have some growing pains at first but our main goals are to provide both practical and emotional support. My name is Kate and I am a licensed counselor here in

Maryland. And I am just recently divorced myself so this will be a great help for me as well. So let's go around the room and give our names and why we are here. Now who would like to start?" Kate wasn't surprised to see Linda's hand shoot up.

It was going to be a long night.

NINE

John picked up the girls for his week, and for once, it was an almost civil exchange. The reasons were made clear when Kate walked out to hand him Emma's sleepover bag and saw Bethany sitting in the passenger seat staring straight ahead as if there was nothing she wanted more than to watch the asphalt in front of her.

Kate seethed for a second then let it go. She couldn't be bothered by it anymore. They deserved each other. Unfortunately, her daughters deserved better, but you played the hand you were dealt.

John took Emma's bag and put it in the back. Kate blew kisses and waved at her girls as he got in and drove away.

When they were out of sight, Kate went back in and stood in her foyer. Since everyone was on vacation, she had cancelled support group for the week. With nowhere to go and nothing to do, she wandered into the family room and pulled a book off the shelf. She had read it before, but she didn't remember what it was about.

She settled into the sofa and started to read.

It was getting dark when she heard a knock at the door. Though neighbors often stopped by for one reason or another, they usually called first. She glanced out the sidelight next to the door and spied a tall, thin figure.

Curious, she turned on the porch light. Patrick smiled at her and gave her a small wave.

Kate swallowed hard then opened the door.

"Hey," he said.

"Hey," she answered.

"I know this is weird but..."

Kate reached out and pulled him into the house.

Patrick pushed the door closed behind him as he pulled her body against his, his lips descending on hers. Kate gasped as his hands moved all over her.

Their kisses grew more urgent as Kate's hands moved under his shirt and up the bare skin of his back. His skin was warmed from the sun, but smooth and dry. When he started to pull her t-shirt up, Kate pulled him into the living room and the two fell onto the couch as their clothes fell away.

Patrick stopped and pulled away, panting. "Are you sure?"

Kate interrupted him again with her lips and pulled him down on top of her.

As Patrick moved over her, Kate inwardly cursed her stupidity. She'd promised herself she wouldn't encourage him and here he was moving inside of her with an urgency she shared. It had been so long that she responded almost immediately and in minutes was already climaxing.

Soon it was Patrick's turn and when he collapsed on top of her, Kate wrapped her arms and legs around him, forcing him deeper into her until their bodies melded into one. Patrick obliged and wrapped his long arms around her.

After a few minutes, Patrick moved to lie beside her and playfully leaned over and nibbled at her breast like they'd been lovers for years and not minutes. Kate pushed up to sit at the end of the couch and pulled her knees up, self-conscious of her aging body. She grabbed the lap blanket off the back of the couch and covered herself.

Patrick pulled it off of her. "Don't," he said. "I think you're perfect."

Kate shook her head then stood up to wrap the blanket around her then walked out of the room.

Patrick jumped up and intercepted her before she could reach the stairs. "Stop. Why do you do that?"

Kate looked away. "I could be your mom," she said miserably.

Patrick laughed. "My mom could be your mom. I have a sister the same age as you are."

That didn't make her feel any better. "I'm too old for you Patrick."

Patrick moved over to her and wrapped his arms around her. Kate rested her forehead against his chest and felt him kiss the top of her head.

"Doesn't it matter what I think?" he whispered, then lifted her chin to press his lips against hers.

TEN

Kate and Patrick spent the better part of the week together. When it was time for the girls to come home and Patrick to leave, she was exhausted. She did a quick cleaning and changed the sheets on everyone's beds. She was just throwing in another load of laundry when she heard a car stop in front of the house.

Kate went downstairs and opened the door to see John walking the girls up the front steps. As before, Bethany sat in the passenger's seat, staring holes in the pavement in front of her. Kate had no clue why the girl looked so angry. She'd gotten everything she wanted after all. Kate decided to ignore her.

"There are my sweet girls!" she cried and held her arms out.

Lizzie and Emma threw their bags into the foyer then wrapped their arms around her hips.

Kate looked up to ask John how things went, but he was already halfway back to the car. She shrugged and let the door close behind her.

"Come on in the kitchen. I made cupcakes!"

"Yay!" Lizzie screamed and ran ahead of them. Emma buried her face in Kate's hip, obviously upset. Kate reached down and picked up her daughter and carried her into the kitchen to set her on a stool at the counter.

"What happened?"

"It was boring," Lizzie announced through a mouthful of icing. "They yell a lot."

Kate reached into the fridge for milk. "What do you mean they yell a lot?"

"Bethany's mad because she thought she was going to live here instead of you, and Daddy told her that he couldn't afford two houses, so she was going to have to go back to work," Emma said quietly.

"She yells the most," Lizzie affirmed.

"Well, pregnant women can get very upset. Their hormones can make them say crazy things." Kate tried to sound nonjudgmental.

Emma shook her head. "She's not going to have a baby anymore. Daddy said she lost it."

"It's 'cause she yells so much," Lizzie said, her mouth still full. "It didn't want to be her baby anymore because it doesn't want a mommy that yells all the time."

Kate was stunned. John hadn't said anything to her about Bethany losing the baby and, to be honest, she was glad. He was the type of person who projected blame on whomever was nearby, regardless of who was really at fault. It would be just like him to hold Kate accountable for things that had nothing to do with her.

"Well, did you at least have a nice time with Daddy?"

Emma shrugged. "I guess."

Kate pulled open the fridge to look for something pull out for dinner later when she heard a knock on the front door.

"I'll get it!" Lizzie ran out of the kitchen with icing all over her face.

Kate followed, wondering if John forgot something.

Lizzie pulled open the front door to reveal Patrick holding up two boxes of pizza. She stared at him, obviously confused about seeing him out of context.

"Are you here to swim with us because we don't have a pool," she said with her preschool logic.

Patrick laughed. "No, I knew your dad was bringing you home, and I thought you might want some pizza for dinner." He stared at Lizzie blocking the doorway with her sturdy little body. "Can I come in?"

"What kind of pizza is it?"

"One is extra cheese, and the other is extra pepperoni and cheese."

"I love extra cheese!" Lizzie yelled and ran back to the kitchen.

"You didn't have to do that," Kate said taking the pizzas.

"I figured you might be kind of tired." He leaned over and gave her a quick kiss.

Kate shivered at the touch of his lips. "Thanks. That was really sweet."

They had already polished off the cheese pizza when Patrick asked, "Did you guys have a good week?"

Kate could tell that Emma wanted to be loyal to her dad but seemed to struggle to find something positive to say.

Lizzie, though, held no qualms about throwing her father under the parenting bus. "No. It was boring. We didn't even go anywhere."

"Oh..." Patrick was nonplussed for a moment. "I thought he might take you to the fair."

Emma shook her head and picked at the wrapper on the cupcake in front of her. "We just stayed inside and watched cartoons."

"Well...then...maybe we should go," Patrick offered.

"Yeah!" Lizzie started bouncing on the barstool. "Yeah yeah yeah! I'm gonna have lemonade, and I'm gonna win a fish, and I'm gonna have a deep fried Oreo..."

"Are we going now?" Emma looked hopeful.

"I think we can make a plan to go..." Kate started to answer.

"I already bought passes for today," Patrick interrupted.

Emma jumped up and wrapped her arms around his neck, then ran to get her shoes on with Lizzie hot on her heels.

"You don't have to do this," Kate said, her voice lowered.

Patrick reached over and entwined his fingers with hers. "I know that. But I want to."

Since Lizzie still rode in a booster seat, Patrick drove Kate's SUV to the fairgrounds. Even late in the day, the parking lot was packed, so Patrick followed the pointing attendants to a spot far from the front gate. Kate knew Lizzie was going to start complaining about the walk, so she stepped around the truck to offer her a piggyback ride. She was surprised to see that Lizzie was already astride Patrick's shoulders.

"Let's go!" she shouted, and they set off.

The fairgrounds were small by most standards, and other than a handful of rides and a few games, the food trucks and exhibition halls took up the rest of the available space.

Since Patrick paid for their entrance admission, Kate bought the ride tickets and sat and watched as they made a circuit of the smaller rides. Both girls seemed to be having a great time, and Patrick was end-lessly patient when they asked to go on certain rides over and over again.

When they had exhausted the novelty of the small roller coasters, the girls announced that they were hungry. To save on complaints, Patrick put Lizzie back on his shoulders and Kate offered her hand to Emma. She was surprised when Patrick took it instead. Suddenly shy, she couldn't look at him and watched in wonder as Emma took his other hand. Lizzie had a death grip around Patrick's neck, and Kate marveled that he could still breathe. To his credit, he seemed perfectly comfort-able as they set off toward the food vendors.

Kate was painfully aware that at any moment someone could come along and see them. No sooner had the thought crossed her mind when she spotted one of her more intrusive neighbors, a woman named Diane, walking toward her with her own children in tow. She knew she'd be the subject of gossip forever if the wrong person came along...and here she was. Kate knew from Michelle that Diane had been in conversations with just about anyone who would listen about Kate's marital problems. She had even brought it up in the volunteer room at the school, which made Kate furious. She dropped Patrick's hand and pulled open her purse to search for something, anything, that could forestall his gestures of familiarity. At the bottom of her bag she found a bottle of hand sanitizer and seized it for the life ring that it was.

"Um, you guys need to clean up before we do anything else. Those rides are filthy," she said by way of explanation.

"Hey!" She heard a voice behind her as she made a show of squeezing copious amounts of goo into Emma's hands. Kate turned to look and was mortified to see Michelle and their other friend, Dawn, coming up behind them with their kids just as Diane was stopping in front of them, her eyebrows up to her hairline. Patrick let a giggling Lizzie fall from his shoulders so that she could get her own gob of hand gel, then took the bottle from Kate to clean off his own hands.

"Wow, it's like a neighborhood reunion," Kate remarked. She could feel her face blazing under Diane's scrutiny. Michelle wasn't a big fan of Diane, so she hung back a bit as if gauging the direction of the conversation. Dawn followed suit.

Instead of responding, Diane peered at Patrick. "Aren't you a lifeguard at our pool?" she asked.

Patrick smiled politely, but Kate could see the muscles in his cheek clench. "I'm actually the facilities manager."

Diane looked skeptical. "They give management jobs to high schoolers?"

"Well, no," Patrick chuckled. "That *would* be impressive, but I've been out of high school for a while now. I'm finishing my masters at College Park."

Kate searched her brain for a way to end the conversation before Diane started questioning him about their relationship. Luckily, Lizzie chose that moment to reassert her comfort as everyone else's primary concern. "I'm thirsty," she announced. "Can we get lemonade now?"

"Sure, we'll all go," Patrick answered. He pulled Lizzie up and placed her back onto his shoulders, then took Emma's hand. "I got this," he said to Kate and walked off with the girls, Michelle's two following close behind. Kate suspected his enthusiasm with the kids had less to do with satisfying Lizzie's thirst and more a desire to avoid Diane's interrogation. Her luck went even further when Diane's kids, Jake, Grace, and Tyler, interrupted their mother to follow Lizzie's cue and started whining for snacks. Annoyed and distracted, Diane let her kids pull her away. Kate's luck continued when Dawn's youngest started clamoring for a bathroom, and they moved on as well.

Kate turned to find Michelle looking at her.

"So," Kate began.

Michelle put up her hand. "Don't bother," she announced. "You don't need to say anything."

Kate exhaled audibly. "I wanted to tell you, but it's not exactly something you can find the words for without sounding pathetic, or desperate...or whatever."

"Seriously, Kate, no judgment here," Michelle reassured her. "If you're happy with your young smokin' hot boyfriend, then I'm happy you have a young smokin' hot boyfriend."

"I don't think I can really call him my boyfriend," Kate ventured.

Michelle snorted. "Uh, his car's been in your driveway for a week. I can think of other things to call him, but let's just stick with boyfriend."

"This is all so weird. I feel like I'm doing something horribly wrong... like I'm a pedophile."

Michelle smirked. "If he were fourteen, sure. Even sixteen. But he's what, twenty-four? Twenty-five?" She shrugged her own answer. "So what? I say, go for it. He's a great guy. The gossips in the neighborhood will talk for about a week, then someone's kid'll get pregnant or another divorce will come up, and you'll be old news."

Kate wanted to thank Michelle but glanced behind her and saw her world just got a little bit worse. John and Bethany were approaching their little group just as Patrick walked up with the kids.

Kate felt a little hand push its way into hers and looked down to see Emma looking up at her, her face a mask of confusion. Lizzie still sat astride Patrick's shoulders, happily licking the sugar from her lemonade cup. When she reached down to offer some to her mother, she noticed her father standing in front of them. Kate cringed when Lizzie's face scrunched up.

"Why did you forget to bring us?" Lizzie asked. Kate thought it was a reasonable question and waited to hear her ex-husband's explanation.

Bethany scowled and looked away, her arms crossed in front of her. It didn't escape Kate's notice that a brand new Louis Vuitton bag hung from her arm. She glanced over at her ex in time to see John's face reveal a split second of guilt that quickly gave way to his more typical passive aggressive smirk.

"Bethany wasn't feeling well, so we came to the fair to cheer her up."

"But we wanted to come to the fair," Lizzie protested. She was not about to let her father off the hook.

"I didn't know you wanted to come," John started but Emma interrupted.

"We asked you to take us," she said, tears threatening to spill from her eyes.

John pasted a fake smile on his face. "Well you're here now!"

"Because Patrick brought us," Lizzie's grip on her father's guilt was tenacious.

John noticed Patrick for the first time, and his smile gave way to confusion. Surprisingly, he didn't question who Patrick was or why his daughter was currently sitting on his shoulders.

"Bethany and I would love to take you on some rides if you want," John offered, but the look of horror and anger on Bethany's face belied the offer.

Emma shook her head then reached out and grabbed Patrick's other hand. Michelle showed her solidarity by taking up position on Patrick's other side and stared daggers at Bethany while her children closed in next to her.

"I want to go home," Emma said quietly.

Kate, who had kept silent during the exchange, reached down and picked her daughter up. "Are you sure?"

Emma nodded.

John forced a smile. "Mommy will take you home then, right? Then Bethany and I will take you someplace fun next time."

"Adventure Park!" Lizzie announced, and Kate quietly chuckled at the look of annoyance that crossed John's face. There was no way Lizzie was going to let him weasel out of taking them to Adventure Park, and John *hated* Adventure Park.

"We'll see you later," Kate said, hiding her smile.

John and Bethany moved off with Michelle staring after them. "I give it another month," she predicted then gathered her own children. "Come on gang. It's getting dark and I didn't bring any mosquito spray."

Kate gave Michelle a grateful smile. "We'll see you tomorrow?" she asked.

"Oh count on it." She smiled at Patrick. "Later, handsome."

Kate watched her friend walk away, happy to have at least one person on her side.

ELEVEN

As the summer progressed, it was just as Michelle predicted. Rumor and speculation about Kate's marital problems gave way to a new scandal in the neighborhood. Ironically, it was Diane who was now providing ample fodder for the neighborhood rumormongers by leaving her husband for the husband of her next door neighbor. Kate was relieved to be somewhat free of the gossip and enormously satisfied that it was Diane in the hot seat now.

She'd just hung up with Michelle and was enjoying a quiet glass of wine on the patio while the girls played on their swing set, when John came around the corner of the house.

"I rang the doorbell, but no one answered, so I figured you guys were back here." He sat down next to her. Kate said nothing. She knew from experience that John hated silence. It was only a matter of time before he'd spit it out.

"So, new man, huh?" he fished.

Kate made a face. It had been weeks since they'd seen each other at the fair. There had to be another reason for his being there.

"You guys been seeing each other long?" he asked, his tone more polite than anything else.

"No, not long."

"He looks young," John said, with more of the passive-aggressive snark she was used to.

"How old is Bethany?" Kate asked, knowing full well the girl just celebrated her twenty-third birthday. Emma had plenty to share about that particular dinner.

John dropped the smirk and looked bleak.

"Yeah, that turned out to be a mistake," he said in a rare moment of honesty.

No shit, Kate thought, but kept it to herself. "Nice purse you bought her," she said instead.

John sighed. "If I didn't know better, I'd think she was with me for my credit card."

Kate snorted, but kept quiet. If John couldn't figure out what made him attractive to a girl like Bethany, it wasn't her job to enlighten him.

"She's not the easiest person to get along with," he continued as he stared at their girls. "I just don't get it. She was like the perfect girl at first. Now she won't do anything. She won't cook anything or clean the condo. She gets completely pissed off if I point out stuff that needs to be done. It's like all she wants to do is shop and go out to eat. She's a completely different person now."

Kate stared at him. "It didn't occur to you that she might have been putting on an act? Manipulating you so she could be the second Mrs. Dr. Richardson?"

"No. It wasn't like that. Or at least it didn't start out like that. It's just...she paid attention to me like she was sincerely interested in how I was and wanted me to be happy. She thought I was funny. She'd be flirty and always had something complimentary to say. I hadn't heard anything nice from you in a long time. It felt good. You know a man needs affection sometimes."

Kate shook her head. "Don't make this my fault, John," she warned.

"Well you didn't," he protested.

"You think *you're* the easiest person to get along with? Well, here's some news, you're not. Your idea of affection was shoving your morning wood in my ass crack then ignoring me until something pissed you off. So if that's all your girlfriend is looking for then that makes you two perfect for each other."

John had the nerve to look surprised. "What do you mean?"

Kate looked away. "I don't want to fight with you, John. We're already divorced, so there's no point in having this conversation."

"No, seriously. I want to know what you mean by *if that's all she's looking for*," he insisted.

Kate sighed. "You have this way about you...as if you're constantly judging other people's performance, and they're always coming up short in your estimation. But, to make matters worse, you always have to tell them, to comment on it. Lots and lots of nitpicking, and when you chip away at someone long enough, there's not enough of them left to give you anything. Then you expect them to bend over backward because you're not feeling like you're getting enough attention. You want to hear something nice? Be nice. You want to be loved? Then love. But you're too busy keeping score to love first. You keep raising the bar on what you think you deserve, yet you dole out based on what you get. Then you're surprised when you don't get anything. It's exhausting being with you."

If Kate had been looking at him, she would have seen John's face go through a range of emotions, from anger, to irritation, to regret.

"I didn't know you felt that way," he said quietly.

"Did you ask?" she responded, then held her hand up, "I'll answer that for you. No, you didn't ask. I told you when I was unhappy but you didn't care. It wasn't until *you* were unhappy that you decided to do something about it. But instead of solving your problem with me, you solved it the way that suited you the best."

"So I guess it's too late for us then, huh?" This time he just looked sad which surprised her. She didn't want to feel sympathy for him.

"We're divorced, John. It was too late long before today," Kate replied harshly. "Go back to Bethany."

It was John's turn to shake his head. "I don't want to. I told her I wasn't going to marry her, but she won't leave the condo...and I can't get her to quit either."

Kate stifled a smile. "So the employee you had an affair with won't let you break up with her and she's still working for you at the practice?"

John looked embarrassed. "She gave me an ultimatum. Either we still get married or else."

Kate wanted to laugh. The girl definitely had some serious balls. "What's the 'else'?" she asked.

John rubbed his face. "I don't know, but I'm sure it'll be bad."

Kate shook her head. "You really screwed yourself on this one, didn't you?"

John looked at her, his face tired. "So, any chance I can come back here? Even if it's just until I get the Bethany thing worked out?"

"No chance. You're just going to have to suck it up and deal with it on your own."

"You know I don't have to let you live here," he sneered. And there it was. Old John had returned.

Kate's eyes narrowed. "You signed the financial settlement already."

John shrugged. "But the judge hasn't signed it. Things change. I could easily call my attorney."

Kate was suddenly furious, but kept her voice steady. "I have a really good friend at church who's an employment attorney. He represents employees in wrongful termination and sexual harassment suits. I could give him a call just as easily."

John stared at her. Kate stared right back.

"Make trouble for me, and I will make trouble for you," she said quietly. "I'm done with you being an asshole to me."

John's face turned red, and Kate braced herself for the attack. Then all the air went out of him.

"I'm sorry," he said quietly to her surprise. "I *am* an asshole, aren't I?"

Kate sat back and took a sip of her wine. "Yes, you are, but the first step to recovery is admitting you have a problem."

John got up and walked over to the girls who greeted their father with hugs. John gave them hugs and kisses and as Kate watched, she wondered if John had ever loved her like that.

TWELVE

Later that night, Kate left for her support group. Michelle had graciously offered to babysit, then extended the invitation to include a sleepover. Lizzie and Emma were thrilled and didn't even look back when Kate dropped them off.

It was a short drive to the church, and Kate arrived early to set up refreshments. She was just setting out the cookies and tea sandwiches when she heard a car drive up. Kate closed her eyes and prayed for patience before turning to greet Linda, her early arrival.

"Oh, is that what we're having...again?" Linda asked with a sniff then stepped away in case Kate was going to ask for help.

"Good evening, Linda," Kate replied, ignoring the comment. "I'm not quite ready yet."

"Oh that's OK. I need to use the lavatory." Linda chirped. Kate shook her head. Only Linda would use a word like lavatory.

She was happy to see two of the other women enter a short time later. Georgia was beautiful in the way old movie stars used to be but had a mouth like a sailor. Kate secretly wondered why she came to the meetings since she didn't seem to be struggling with anything. She was followed by Rebecca, who Kate didn't know well yet. Rebecca was shy and obviously struggling with something. Kate hoped she would grow to trust the group enough to share her concerns.

She was setting up the coffee when a new face appeared in the doorway and asked, "Am I in the right place?"

Georgia turned to her. "If you're a woman, yes, you are, and come right in. If you're a man, you can turn around and go fu..."

Kate cut her off. "Georgia! Let's watch our language here, please."

The very beautiful Georgia threw her hair over her shoulder in a huff. "Oh give it up, Kate. It's not like we're in the church or anything."

Kate gave Georgia a stern look as she crossed the room to the new woman. "I'm sorry about that. Don't mind Georgia. She's still dealing with some anger issues." She held out her hand. "Hi, I'm Kate. I'm the facilitator for this group. Am I right in guessing that you're Judith?"

Judith gave her a nervous smile. "Hi. Yes, I'm Judith."

Kate beamed at her and, while still holding her hand, led Judith into the room. "Well, Judith, let me introduce you to our early arrivals. This is Rebecca. She's been with us for three meetings now, so she's still a bit of a newbie." Rebecca gave Judith a small smile and a brief wave. "And, as you might have already guessed, this is Georgia. While I wouldn't call her a newbie, since she's been with us for a few meetings, she's not quite one of our veterans either." At this, Georgia snorted and rolled her eyes. Kate ignored her and nodded at the coffee table. "Why don't you help yourself to something and have a seat. We're expecting three more tonight. Snacks are homemade, and coffee's always decaf. I'll be right back." Kate gave her hand a reassuring squeeze and left the room just as Linda was entering the front door. Kate turned away and hurried down the hall.

Her phone was buzzing, and Kate worried that it was Michelle trying to reach her. She stepped into the nearby small office and pulled her phone out. Instead of a call, Patrick had sent her a text full of hearts. She smiled, then sent one back and reset her phone so that it would chirp if Michelle called and vibrate if Patrick called. She was about to put her phone away when it vibrated again. Kate laughed to herself and took a moment to respond to Patrick's text...then all the others following it. Mindful of the time, she finally put her phone away and started assembling the handouts the church had put together when Linda appeared in the doorway.

"There you are!" she cried. "I wanted a chance to speak with you privately to let you know that I've been volunteering as an assistant at the preschool and I feel with my experiences...well, I could certainly step in if you ever needed a break." Linda's expression was earnest. Kate stared at her for a moment, realizing that the woman standing in front of her actually felt her work with three-year-olds qualified her to counsel women going through a divorce. Linda continued on in that vein for several more minutes until Kate finally had to interrupt her.

"You'll have to take that up with the church, Linda. They're the ones that assign counselors to groups." She moved past Linda to return to the meeting room. Linda followed.

"Oh, OK, I can certainly do that. I just thought that maybe unofficially...Megan!" Linda cried as she stepped around Kate. "I was saving that seat! I had my handbag there and everything!"

Kate watched as Georgia reached over, plucked Linda's patchwork handbag off the floor at Megan's feet and threw it at Linda. "There, then," Georgia snapped. "There's your damn handbag. Now, go sit over there and shut it."

Linda looked like she was about to chuck her handbag, not at Georgia, but at Megan for taking her seat. Georgia caught Linda's glare at Megan and was about to speak when Kate interrupted her.

"Now, now, ladies." She placed herself between Linda and the rest of the group. "Let's take our seats and get acquainted with our new member. We don't want to give her a bad impression of us on her first day, do we?"

"Too late," Georgia chimed. Linda shot a venomous look at Megan and took the last seat in the semicircle. Kate waited until she had settled before addressing the group.

"So, why don't I give Judith a little bit of my history, and then we'll move to Rebecca and work our way down."

Kate took a deep breath then began. Unfortunately what had started out so promising had turned into yet another episode of the Linda show. It felt like hours had passed since anyone but Linda had spoken.

"Very informative," Kate said then looked at her watch. "Well, how about we take a fifteen-minute break then regroup?" She glanced around at the dead expressions. "Let's make that twenty minutes, then we'll see if Judith is ready to share."

Kate got up and left the room, ostensibly for the restroom, with Linda following. She had hoped to have at least a second to pee, but Linda kept up right behind her.

Kate stopped just outside the bathroom door and faced Linda.

"...and I think a twenty-minute break is far too long. We don't want the ladies feeling neglected, do we?" Linda pestered.

Kate took a deep breath. "The point of the break is to allow the women to develop supportive friendships with each other. That's difficult to do during session, so my intention is to allow them the time to speak with each other more personally. Now, if you'll excuse me," Kate, ignoring Linda's protests, pushed through the bathroom door and locked it.

Thank God it was a single bathroom and not one with stalls, or Linda would have followed her in there. As it was, she could hear Linda just outside the door having a conversation with the wood. Kate ignored her and pulled out her phone. Patrick had been texting her during the meeting. Several were comical selfies and some surprisingly loving texts. Trying not to laugh, she answered several of the texts, but eschewed any photos in favor of written flirtations. Since Michelle had the girls for the evening, Patrick had obviously let himself in, and from the background, it looked like Patrick was taking photos of himself in her bed.

One text gave her pause. It wasn't from Patrick, and it wasn't from anyone on her contact list. Kate pulled it up. "You know you really shouldn't be messing around with that kid," it read.

Kate's initial reaction was confusion at first, then annoyance. John must have bought a new phone. Rather than answer in kind, Kate took the high road and deleted it without sending a response. Just then, another dirty selfie from Patrick popped up, and Kate completely forgot about the other text.

Her time was almost up, so she took a quick picture of her lips pursed in a kiss and sent it to him. Linda was still just outside the door and still talking, though Kate had no idea about what. She pretended to listen as she made her way back into the meeting room, where Linda continued talking nonstop all the way back to her chair.

Kate gave them all a tired smile. "So, Judith. Do you feel ready to share yet?"

"Um, sure," Judith stammered. "But I'm not quite sure how to start."

"Why don't you tell us what you're feeling now?" Kate offered. "What brought you tonight?"

"Well, I'm tired." Judith joked, and everyone, except Linda, laughed. "And I'm here because my friend, Susan, thinks I need more like-minded friends. That's it, I guess. I'm not sure I'm ready for anything deeper than that."

"Well, that's a good start, Judith. I hope we'll see you next week then." Kate looked at her watch. "I know it seems like I'm cutting you short, but we're actually out of time for tonight. Are there any sugges-tions for next week's meeting?"

"I've got one," Georgia piped up. "How about we dispense with the tea and have some wine and cheese instead?" This suggestion drew quiet cheers from the other women.

Kate smiled and shook her head. "I'm sorry. As nice as that sounds, our goal is to eliminate crutches, not build them." Her words were met with groans, but she held firm.

Georgia put up her hands. "Sorry, ladies. I tried."

"Well, I wish you all a great week. I'll see you here, same time same place next week. Shall we?"

Kate stood and held out her hands, then waited as everyone came together and bowed their heads. "Dear Lord," she began. "Grant me the strength to change the things that I can, to accept the things I cannot change, and the wisdom to know the difference. Amen."

She looked up to see everyone hugging. She gave her own hugs then went to clean up the refreshments. It was the one thing Linda wouldn't help with, so she knew she'd be left alone. She glanced up to see Linda making a beeline for Georgia and silently wished the other woman well.

It was late by the time she got home, and she was surprised that the house was completely dark. She was sure Patrick had taken the photos there, but the house looked empty. She let herself in and locked the door behind her. As her eyes adjusted to the dark, she could sense a glow coming from the stairs. Dropping her keys and bag on the table next to the door, she followed the light up the stairs to her bedroom, where Patrick had lit what looked like every candle she owned. The whole room was aglow with candlelight, and Patrick lay on her bed, completely nude, his body bathed in the glow. He was asleep.

Smiling, Kate peeled off her clothes and crawled up from the foot of the bed. Patrick barely stirred as she gently moved against him then his eyes flew open and he graced her with one of his dazzling smiles then rolled over on top of her. Kate marveled at the feeling of his warm body against hers and in no time they were climaxing together. She wrapped her legs around him as he fell against her, panting. She loved the weight of his body on hers. After a moment, she could feel him kissing her on her shoulder, then felt bereft when he lifted himself off of her to trail kisses down her belly.

"This is how I want to die," he panted against her back, and Kate smiled.

"Naked?" she asked.

She could feel Patrick's smile against her skin.

"No, inside you," he replied.

Spent, Kate and Patrick curled against each other under the covers. Though sexually satiated, Kate couldn't sleep. She enjoyed the feeling of Patrick's warm body curved against hers, his hand cradling her breast. She lay, feeling the rise and fall of his breath and watched the candles sputter out one by one. She thought Patrick was sleeping when he spoke.

"I want to take you out to dinner," he said against her neck, his breath tickling the tiny hairs at the bottom of her hairline.

Kate turned to look at him. "You want to take me out? Like *out* out?"

Patrick nuzzled her ear. "Yes *out* out. Why? Don't you want to go out?"

Kate considered that for a moment. "I guess I never thought about it. Wouldn't you be uncomfortable being out with me?"

Patrick pulled back and frowned at her. "Why would you ask that?"

Kate shrugged. "I don't know. I just thought you might feel weird... that people might talk...or comment."

Patrick's lip curled in a half-smile that Kate found so adorable she wanted to kiss it. "I'm counting on people commenting. They'll say, 'Look at the guy with the amazingly sexy girlfriend. I wonder how he got her.' You're going to raise my street cred."

Kate smiled in spite of herself. "Yeah right, more like 'isn't that his mother?' I don't want to embarrass you."

"Oh please. Do you even know how beautiful you are? There's no way you could embarrass me. You should be embarrassed *of* me...You're way out of my league."

Kate stared at him. His tone sounded light, but his expression was serious.

"You know it wasn't a question anyway," he said, as he pressed kisses all along her collarbone. "I'm going to take you out, whether you like it or not."

Kate smiled at him then watched him fall asleep.

THIRTEEN

Their date had to wait until the girls were with their dad, and Kate was secretly glad for the delay. She still felt very conflicted about going out on an actual date with Patrick. It really wasn't about what people might say, like she'd said to Patrick. It was more that if she embarrassed him, it might change the way he felt about her. In the privacy of her own home, they weren't defined by their ages, but out in public, she felt like their age difference would be glaringly obvious. And she'd never really thought about them having a relationship outside the bedroom.

It didn't help that John kept sending her idiotic, none-of-his-business texts about her relationship with Patrick. Though he kept them relatively benign, they were irritating for their assumption that she would care what he thought about her dating life. Kate wished the act of deleting them was as satisfying as slamming a door. Just tapping her screen didn't quite have the same emotional impact. Her impending date with Patrick was causing her so much stress she wanted to take it out on something.

She really needed to talk to someone, and this wasn't the kind of issue to bring up in her support group.

Of all the people she knew, only Michelle would understand her dilemma without judgment...or with minimal judgment, at least. She invited Michelle and her brood over for sprinklers and popsicles and hoped her subterfuge wasn't glaringly obvious.

They sat out on the patio with margaritas in hand. Michelle shifted to look her square in the face.

Kate was nonplussed. "What?"

"Spill it," Michelle ordered. "I know you've got something on your chest, so spill it."

Kate took a big sip of her drink. "Patrick wants to take me out to dinner."

"Is there more, or is that it?"

"That's it, I guess." Embarrassed, Kate looked away.

Michelle looked confused. "I'm sorry but I think I'm missing something. Was there an issue in there somewhere...or a question?"

Kate sighed. "I don't know how comfortable I am with the idea of publicly dating him."

"Why? Is he secretly gross...like farts at the dinner table gross?"

Kate laughed. "No, nothing like that. It's just the age thing. I feel like people are going to look at me weird."

"Since when do you care what other people think?" Michelle asked.

"I care what *he* thinks," Kate answered. "I feel like when he realizes what other people will think...it'll be over."

Michelle snorted into her drink. "If it's that easy to change his mind about you, I say good riddance. Have you thought about what *you* want from this relationship?"

"What do you mean?" Kate pretended not to understand, but Michelle wasn't buying it.

"You're a big girl. I'm sure you've thought ahead. What do you want with him next week, or next year? Or even ten years from now? If it's just about the sex..." Michelle put her hand up before Kate could protest. "I'm not stupid, Kate. You guys are bangin' like rabbits, and that's OK. But is that all you want? You have to ask yourself if this is just a fling for now or a relationship forever. Once you figure out what you want, then you need to talk to him about what he wants."

"He wants to die with his...um, his...inside me," Kate said dully.

Michelle laughed out loud. "God, that's so romantic. But seriously, you two need to get on the same page...and soon."

"I don't know if I'm ready for that," Kate admitted. "I haven't really thought past this date."

Michelle shrugged. "Then go on the date, and see what happens."

Michelle got up to refill their glasses. Kate watched the kids running around the yard. She knew Michelle was right. She just didn't know what to do about it.

Kate knew she couldn't avoid the date any longer after John took the girls for his weekend. Patrick had been dropping not so subtle hints that he had big things planned for them and told her in no uncertain terms that they were going out that weekend.

Since it was a surprise, Kate had no idea what to wear. It was a struggle to find something that didn't scream "mom" and equally difficult to not dress like she was desperately trying to look young. Patrick had only suggested that she look "nice." She was about to give up when she found a sleeveless cotton dress that she'd bought a couple of years before at Banana Republic. It was nice enough to wear with heels, but casual enough to pair with flip-flops. She compromised and wore her Tory Burch flip-flops so she'd be appropriate no matter where they went. Kate pulled her hair into a ponytail and grabbed a small Kate Spade clutch. She knew her look fell somewhere between expensive soccer mom and expensive co-ed.

When Patrick arrived to pick her up, she knew she'd chosen well. He was casual in fitted khaki pants and a light blue short-sleeved button down that he'd left untucked. He looked like he'd be at home anywhere.

He whistled when she opened the door.

"Wow," he said with a big smile. "You look amazing. You ready to go?"

Kate nodded. She felt weirdly thrilled as Patrick walked her to his ancient BMW. Like a gentleman, he opened her door and then got in behind the wheel.

"Where are we going?" she asked.

Patrick gave her another dazzling smile. "Well, we're going to one of my favorite restaurants first, then there's a surprise for after dinner."

Kate wondered what kind of restaurants twenty-five-year-olds loved. She was thankful they were passing all the pizza places and fast food joints on their drive into Baltimore. They parked in one of the garages downtown and started to walk. Patrick had her close her eyes and told her to open them when they stopped.

She looked up to see that they were at The Brewer's Art, and her esteem of Patrick rose considerably.

"We're eating here?" she asked. "This is wonderful! I've always wanted to come here!"

Patrick looked visibly relieved. "I was a little worried," he admitted. "I think I'm the only one in my family who's a fan of their house beer. I'm a little obsessed with craft brews right now, so it's awesome that you're willing to come here with me."

Patrick pulled her close and gently kissed her on the lips. "Are you ready?"

Kate nodded.

As expected, The Brewer's Art turned out to be amazing. The food was exceptional and, though she was more a wine drinker, the beer was phenomenal. Better, the crowd in the restaurant was an eclectic mix of young and old foodies and beer connoisseurs, and Kate felt gratifyingly invisible.

It was still light out when they were done, so Patrick took her hand and they walked the distance back toward the parking garage. Instead of heading to Patrick's car, he steered her into the Meyerhoff Symphony Hall.

"We're going here?" If she was invisible at the restaurant, Kate found herself sticking out like a sore thumb as they navigated the sea of elderly symphony patrons. One well-dressed, well-cared for woman in particular gave Patrick an obvious once over, then nodded at Kate approvingly.

Kate was impressed. Their seats were excellent, and when the conductor announced the show, she knew Patrick had gone to great lengths to please her. They would be watching an airing of *Casablanca* that was to be scored by the BSO itself.

Kate could tell that Patrick was very pleased with himself. "Did you do all this for me?" she asked.

"Not even," Patrick retorted then took her hand in his. "Bogart's my boy. Have you seen him in *The Desperate Hours*? Dude's a badass."

The movie was amazing. Kate hadn't seen it since college, and the addition of the symphony created the most incredible surround sound effect ever. Every emotion on the screen was infused with nuances in the musical score made larger by the full symphony in front of them. It was almost overwhelming, and Kate saw several women wiping their eyes. That Patrick had thought to bring her to something John would never have thought of spoke volumes about him.

When it was done, there was a collective sigh of satisfaction that ran through the audience. The applause was thunderous. Kate's face hurt from all the smiling.

Patrick took her hand and led her out of the hall past the slower moving patrons.

"Wasn't that insane?" he asked when they stopped at the crosswalk that led to their parking garage. Kate was about to answer when they heard a voice near them.

"Oh my God, Patrick?"

Kate turned to see two girls about Patrick's age walking up to them. Except for their hair color, they could have been twins with their generous figures stuffed into almost identical Herve Leger knock-off bandage dresses. Their heels were so high they could barely walk.

Patrick grimaced. "Oh hey, Lily...hey, Kara."

Kate moved aside as the girls rushed forward and made a great show of giving Patrick hugs. For his part, his response was half-hearted at best.

"What are you doing here?" the blond one asked, pointedly ignoring Kate.

"We just saw *Casablanca*," Patrick answered, his eye over her shoulder. He seemed to be longing for the parking garage.

The dark-haired girl finally noticed Kate. "Oh my God, you took your mom to see a movie? That is so nice!" she cried with unfortunate sincerity.

Patrick winced. "Um, this isn't my mom, Kara. This is Kate, my girlfriend."

Both girls turned and stared at Kate. She felt herself growing hot with anger at the unflattering scrutiny. It was exactly what she had been afraid of.

"Seriously?" said one, and "Oh...sorry," said the other. Then both turned to give Patrick their full attention.

"So, we're going to Owl Bar. You want to come? Todd, Kimmie, and Matt are meeting us there," the blond one said in a rush. "You *have* to come. It'll be so much fun."

Patrick murmured something and shook his head, then moved to pull Kate away, but the blonde grabbed his other arm and made a great show of stopping him. Kate began to seethe, but held her tongue. These were Patrick's friends, and she didn't want to pitch a fit in front of them.

"Come *on,* Patrick. It'll be like a reunion! You're mom...I mean your girlfriend can go if she wants to. We'll give you a ride later."

Kate felt the top of her head explode and walked away before she slapped someone.

"See, she's fine with it," she heard someone say behind her. She picked up her pace so she wouldn't have to hear the rest.

Once inside the parking garage, Kate's eyes burned at the overwhelming stench of urine from the thousands of homeless people who had made it their home at one time or another. It matched her mood perfectly. Not caring about her dress, she leaned against the wall to catch her breath and then dug out her cell phone. She was so angry, she couldn't see the screen to dial for a cab. She could feel her heart pounding in her chest and knew tears were next when a hand reached out and took her phone from her.

"Don't," he said quietly. Patrick put his arms around her. "Please don't. I'm sorry...I'm sooo sorry. They're total assholes. Please don't let them upset you."

Kate pressed her face to his chest for a moment and inhaled the sweet sun smell of him. She could feel her heart calm its angry beat, and the anger drain from her. It was like Patrick aromatherapy. She took another breath and stepped out of his arms. She didn't want to, but knew she had no choice. It truly wasn't meant to be.

"Go," she said quietly. "Go with them. I'll find my way home."

Patrick looked at her. "I'm not going anywhere with them. I didn't like them in high school, and I didn't like them in college. They are shallow, empty-headed morons with no other ambition than to find a husband, so they can shop and gossip for the rest of their lives."

"They act like they're your friends," Kate countered.

Patrick shrugged. "I dated Kara for a little while, but it wasn't anything. The ones they're meeting, Todd and Matt, are my friends, but I can catch up with them anytime," he replied. "They'll probably ditch Lily and Kara as soon as they can. Please, Kate. Please don't be upset. I hate to see you like this."

Kate shook her head and looked away. Shame and sorrow filled her heart and it was her own fault. She couldn't tie Patrick down to a life she'd already started. He deserved a chance to have all the moments she'd already had.

"Come on," he said grabbing her hand and pulling her toward the car. "Let's go home."

Kate let herself be led to the car and said nothing when he opened her door. She had little to say on the drive home and met his attempts at small talk with silence.

When they arrived at her house, she let herself out rather than wait for Patrick to open her door and quickly made her way up her steps to the front door.

"Kate...wait," he called as she unlocked her door and stepped inside. Kate turned and looked at him. She could tell he felt terrible...as terrible as she felt.

"Go home Patrick...or go out. It doesn't matter. This was a stupid idea. I don't know what I was thinking."

"What do you mean?" he asked.

"We're just too far apart...for this," she said.

"For what?" he asked. He could tell he was forestalling the inevitable.

"For us," she answered. "I have to go." Kate turned away and closed the door behind her.

She waited for a moment, knowing that Patrick hadn't left. She could see him through the curtained sidelight and knew that he put his hand up to knock several times before turning away and walking back to his car.

It wasn't until he drove away that Kate let the tears fall. She ignored the ping in her bag telling her she'd received another text.

FOURTEEN

The next day Michelle stopped by to fake borrow something so she could find out about Kate's date the night before. When Kate opened the door, Michelle stood on her step holding out an empty measuring cup. It made her chuckle, and she was glad for the effort.

"So?" Michelle asked as she followed Kate into the kitchen. "How was it?"

"Disastrous." She poured Michelle a cup of coffee.

Michelle took a seat at the counter. "I knew it. He's a table farter, isn't he?"

Kate laughed again. "No. That part was great. We went to eat at The Brewer's Art then he took me to see *Casablanca* at the Meyerhoff."

Michelle looked impressed. "Really? That sounds kind of awesome. What did he do, talk during the whole movie?"

Kate's face fell, and she shook her head. "No...all of that was wonderful. It's just that, when we were leaving, we ran into some girls he went to high school with...or dated...or whatever. Anyway, they thought I was his mother."

Michelle stared at her for a second. "Are you serious? Come on, Kate. You can't be upset over something like that."

"It was mortifying," Kate insisted. "They acted like I was invisible."

Michelle looked skeptical. "First, girls like that are too shallow to know how old or how young you really are. If you were only a couple of years older, they would have said the same thing. They were just being stupidly mean. And since when do you care what girls like that think anyway?"

"I don't care what they think," Kate answered. "The point is they're right."

"Uh...No, they're not," Michelle said. "There's more to this than what some bubble heads think. Now, what's really going on?"

Kate sighed. "It's just that there's too much difference between us right now and I don't mean just in age. I've already done everything... dating...marriage...having babies. I've lived through all the firsts. He hasn't. If this is anything more than a fling, he's giving up all of that. I just can't do that to him."

"And *is* this more than a fling?" Michelle asked. Kate turned her face away, embarrassed. "It is, isn't it? You have feelings for him, don't you?"

Kate didn't answer but gave a slight nod and blushed a deep red.

"Oh my God, you love him! But that's a *good* thing!"

"First, I don't know if I love him, and second, no, it isn't a good thing. What kind of future would we have? Even if he did feel the same way, which I'm sure he doesn't."

Michelle gave her a look of pity. "You're thinking about this too much. Have you even asked him what he thinks about all of this, or are you two too busy getting to know each other?"

Kate stared into her mug. "The truth is, I haven't asked him. I think I'm too afraid of the answer."

"But what if the answer is something good? Something you want to hear?" Michelle pressed.

"I can't be the reason he has to quick-start his life."

"Then he can't win either way, can he?"

Kate looked at her friend and knew it was true.

"No," she answered. "He can't."

FIFTEEN

As if things couldn't get worse, John was in a foul mood when he and Bethany dropped off the girls that afternoon. Lizzie and Emma both looked withdrawn and frightened when Kate opened the door. She was instantly furious and ushered the girls into the house before confronting John about it. Instead, he launched into her.

"This visit schedule you cooked up is complete bullshit, you know," he snapped. "You're forcing our girls to stay in a cramped bedroom for a weekend, or even a week at a time, while you get to practically vacation here with your boyfriend."

"What are you talking about?" Kate was shocked. "This is what you agreed to, and this is what the judge signed."

"You thought I wouldn't figure out your game, did you?" he snapped. "You're trying to pin this whole thing on me and Bethany, when the whole time you were fucking that boy toy."

"Are you serious?" Kate was incredulous. "For one thing, a boy toy is a plaything for a *boy,* like your fuckwit in the car there. And second, you're the one who got your boy toy pregnant! I didn't start seeing Patrick until *after* we were divorced! You have no right to come here and attack me like this."

"I have every right," John was in full rant. "This is my house that you've parked your ass in, eating bonbons and watching TV all day while I have to sit in a cramped condo! Worse, your children have to sit in it too just so you can keep the house that I paid for!"

"Are you fucking kidding me? I paid you half the value of this house, and I pay half the mortgage. That was part of the settlement that you agreed to. You didn't give anything away and you don't get to change things now."

John threw the girls' things at her. "We'll see about that," he snapped, then walked back to his car while Bethany smirked in the passenger's seat. With a slam of his car door, John gunned the engine and drove away.

Kate went back inside. Lizzie and Emma were huddled together in the foyer. She dropped to her knees, as Lizzie burst into tears.

"I'm sorry. Mommy's so sorry," she murmured and took them into her arms. "Daddy's just stressed out."

Emma shook her head. Her face was red, but Kate could tell she was trying to be a big girl and not cry. "He's mean. He and Bethany were yelling the whole time and saying really bad words. And...and...she said she didn't want us to come anymore and...we don't *want* to go there anymore."

Kate was furious. John and his bitch had no right to upset her girls like this. Kate put her anger aside and picked up Lizzie and Emma and carried them into the family room. She set them down with her on the couch.

"Come on," she said quietly. "Let's have a honey pile."

Lizzie buried her face into Kate's neck and continued to sob, while Emma leaned into her side and closed her eyes, silent sobs hitching in her small chest. Soon, they were both calmer, and Kate felt OK about getting up and putting in a DVD. The girls settled in to watch *Tangled* with cookies and milk, while Kate went to call her attorney.

Mercifully, John skipped his weekend with the girls the following week and Kate had thought his ire from the previous week had died down until she received a hearing notice to determine custody modification. When she opened the envelope, she could feel the rage filling her body. John was trying to trump her request for sole custody with one of his own. Unfortunately for her, he filed first and from the looks of the paperwork, he'd filed before their fight in front of the house. She stood next to her mailbox with her hand on her forehead. She tried to calm down. When she looked up, Patrick stood next to his car in the rec center parking lot. He tentatively raised his hand then let it drop to his side. Kate lifted her fingers in a half-hearted wave, this time the ache of longing taking the place of her anger. She turned and walked back into the house.

John had asked to expedite the custody modification but the court granted Kate time to prepare a response. At Kate's request, the court had assigned an attorney to serve as Guardian Ad Litem, or GAL, for the children. The GAL wasted no time determining that the environment with John was too toxic for them and suggested a reduction in visitation.

On the day of the hearing, she felt ready to go to battle with her ex. Though John came prepared, the judge agreed with Kate and more importantly the GAL and ruled to reduce John's visitation. It helped Kate's cause that Bethany chose to accept the ruling with less grace than appropriate and started yelling that Kate could keep the kids but get out of the house. John's entire petition was summarily dismissed and the judge ruled in Kate's favor.

Kate thought the whole thing was over but, unfortunately, John's attorney filed an appeal requesting a change in the GAL. She left the courtroom with a splitting headache. It didn't help that her phone kept pinging her with texts. Not interested in their content, Kate deleted them without reading any of them.

That weekend was John's weekend, and Kate sent her girls off with trepidation. Lizzie had asked for one of Kate's t-shirts to sleep in so Kate packed an old, faded concert shirt that Lizzie loved. She'd given Emma a kid's cell phone with her phone number and the GAL's phone number programmed into it. She warned Emma to keep the phone away from her father and Bethany and to use it only in an emergency. Emma promised and hid the phone deep inside her overnight bag.

For Kate it was the longest weekend of her life, but her phone didn't ring. She counted that as a success though John still found the time to text her admonishing messages about Patrick. When the girls came home, John was still silent but decidedly lacking the hostility he'd shown earlier. Emma and Lizzie were subdued. Bethany was mercifully absent. Kate wanted to confront John about the text messages but knew it would only ignite another argument and upset the girls. Kate gave them lots of love instead and put them to bed early hoping that a good night's rest would make them feel better. The next morning, she made them pancakes and offered to take them shopping for back-to-school clothes. Lizzie was especially excited since she would be starting kindergarten and wanted to look the part.

By the time they got home, the girls were shopped out but happy again. Kate put them to bed and was settling down for the night when the front doorbell rang. She pulled a robe around her and went downstairs.

Kate was puzzled. Though it was early by adult standards, it was late for a neighborhood drop-in visit. She peered through the sidelight and saw two uniforms. Opening the door, she was surprised to see two county sheriff's deputies standing on her front steps. One was older with the bearing of a former member of the military, while the other looked like he'd just stepped out of a fraternity house. Kate could see two more patrol cars behind them.

"Is something wrong?" she asked, worried that something had happened to Michelle or one of the kids.

"Kate Richardson?" the older one asked though it didn't sound like a question.

"Yes?"

"May we come in, please?"

"Oh, of course, I'm sorry." She opened the door wide. The two men filed into her house and waited for her to close the door behind them.

"Is there a place we can sit?" he asked and this time it was a question.

"Yes, we can go into the kitchen...or the family room might be more comfortable," she answered.

"The kitchen is fine," the officer said. He held his hand out for her to lead the way.

They followed her to the small eating area off the kitchen and sat down with her.

"Is someone hurt?" she asked. Kate was starting to get seriously worried.

"Mrs. Richardson, would you be able to tell us where you were last evening?"

Kate was confused. "I was here with my children. Their dad dropped them off yesterday afternoon and we had dinner then I put them to bed. Why?"

Kate watched the two men look at each other as the older one took notes.

"Did you leave the house after you put your daughters to bed?"

Kate was puzzled. "No, of course not," she answered. "Can you please tell me why you're here?"

The older officer sighed. "Your husband..." he began.

"My *ex*-husband," she interrupted. "I'm sorry, but he's my ex-husband. We're divorced."

The officer nodded. "Your ex-husband was found dead this morning by his girlfriend." Both men were watching her keenly.

Kate put her hand to her mouth to stifle a sob. "Oh my God," she choked. "What happened?"

"It appears he was murdered some time late last night."

Kate felt her face go cold while a thick pressure built behind her eyes and a tightness gripped her throat. It was a good thing she was sitting down or she might have found herself on the floor with no one but two disinterested police officers staring at her. As it was she gripped the edge of the cushion beneath her and stared at the wall in front of her without actually seeing it. Then her eyes began to burn and she realized she was crying. Kate raised her hand to her face and covered her eyes.

"Oh my God, oh my God," she moaned as tears started to spill.

"Mrs. Richardson," he began, "we're going to need to ask you to come in for questioning."

Kate looked up. "What? Why?" Through her tears, she could see the older officer's look of dispassionate interest give way to a more calculating scrutiny.

"Mr. Richardson's girlfriend, Bethany Stephens, has informed us that you and your ex-husband recently had an altercation over..." he paused and glanced down at his notepad, "custody issues?"

"You can't possibly think I had anything to do with this...Do you?"

"There are some questions that we just need to clear up. That's all," he replied. "Is there someone you can call to stay with your girls?"

"What...*now*?" Kate asked, and the older officer nodded soberly. Kate stood up and went to the phone, but instead of calling Michelle, she phoned their neighbor, Doug, who was a former state police investigator turned attorney. Kate could barely speak but managed to communicate the situation.

"Don't say anything else," he ordered. "I'll be right there."

Kate then called Michelle, who promised to come over right then. Kate was about to sit down when she heard a quiet knock on the front door. Both had arrived at the exact same time.

Doug introduced himself to the officers and advised them that Kate would not be answering any further questions until he had an opportunity to speak with her. The officers gave each other knowing looks, then handed Doug their contact information and left.

Michelle poured Kate a glass of wine and one for herself as Doug took a seat.

"First, I just want to say how sorry I am that you have to go through this," he said. "Christine wants me to let you know that if you need anything at all, help with the girls, or anything really, to give us a call right away."

Kate nodded, tears threatening to spill again. "Thank you," she whispered.

"Secondly, my specialty is more white collar crime, so if you want me to continue to represent you, I might have to bring in a colleague of mine, Tim Parsons, but we'll wait on that until we see where the investigation goes. OK?"

Kate nodded again, and Doug mirrored her nod this time. "OK, how about filling me in from the beginning. I'm a little out of the loop as far as neighborhood gossip goes." Doug had come with a notebook and opened it to take notes.

Kate took a deep breath. "It started the beginning of summer. I came home to find John here early. He...he...had been having an affair with his hygienist, Bethany Stephens, and he'd gotten her pregnant."

Doug interrupted. "Do you know how long he'd been sleeping with her?"

Kate shook her head. "No. She's only been working for him for about a year, so less than that."

Doug nodded and wrote something down. "And then what happened?"

"I think he planned on staying here, but I told him that he needed to leave. It was ugly, but he packed up some of his things and moved out."

"Do you know where he moved to?" Doug asked as he wrote.

"He bought a condo in Amber Woods," she answered. "Bethany moved in with him and I know the girls share a bedroom there."

"Have you been there?"

Kate shook her head. "I don't even know where it is...I mean the condo itself. I know where complex is."

"So you've never been inside," he stated, and Kate shook her head again.

"He always picks up and drops off here."

Doug took some more notes, and Kate sat silently for a moment. Michelle reached over and took her hand.

"So, tell me about the divorce and the custody issue."

Kate rubbed her eyes and sighed then recounted the humiliating story of her divorce.

"Then what happened?"

"The girls came home from one of his weekends and told me Bethany lost the baby and that she was mad because she thought John would get the house in the divorce."

Doug looked up with a look of derision on his face. "She really thought a judge would give him everything?"

Kate shrugged. "She's dumb and greedy. Who knows what she thought? Anyway, John came by sometime later and admitted that it was a mistake and asked to come back until he got his situation with Bethany sorted out."

Doug shook his head in disbelief. "And what did you say?"

"I told him no," she answered. "He got mad and threatened to call his attorney to rescind the financial agreement."

"And your response?"

"I told him I would give Bethany the name and number of an employment attorney who specialized in sexual harassment and wrongful termination."

Michelle laughed, but Doug held up his hand. "Wait," he said. "Do you mean to tell me the girl was still working for him?"

Kate nodded. "As far as I know."

"Insane," he muttered. "So, what happened after that?"

Kate had to think for a moment. "I petitioned the court to assign a GAL to represent the girls. His name is David Hamilton. He's a family attorney. He testified that the environment at John's was overly stressful for the girls and recommended the current order stay or be modified to reduce John's time with them. Then I got a hearing notice to determine a modification of the custody order."

"And how did that go over?"

Kate made a face. "Badly. Bethany made a scene in the courtroom and was escorted out, and the judge threw out the petition. John has already filed an appeal."

"What is that about, do you think?" Doug asked.

"I think, and this is only a guess, that Bethany either lied or got pregnant on purpose because she wanted to be a dentist's wife...that she thought she'd just come in and take my place. She didn't count on the fact that the state doesn't look kindly on men who abandon their families, so now she's insisting that John be assigned full custody. She seems convinced that if he has the girls, she can live here, and I would have to leave."

"And she thought that would work?"

Kate nodded. "I think John thought it would too. I'm not sure how much is coming from him, or if it's all coming from Bethany, but he accused me of living here like I was on a permanent vacation and threatened to have me kicked out of the house."

Doug nodded. "I heard about that."

Kate looked alarmed and embarrassed. Tears threatened to flow again.

Doug moved to comfort her. "Not like that. Your neighbor, Jeff, from across the street brought it up at the last Neighborhood Watch meeting. I guess John was pretty loud and abusive. We were worried we might need to get involved if you decided to file a restraining order."

Kate put her hands over her eyes. "Oh God," she moaned. "How could this have happened?"

Doug shifted uncomfortably. "I need to ask you, Kate. Did you have anything to do with his death?"

Kate shook her head. "No, I would never. He's still Emma and Lizzie's father, despite our problems." She dropped her hands and looked at Doug, her expression earnest. "You have to believe me."

Doug put down his pen and took her hands. "I do believe you and for one very compelling reason. This entire time you've never used the past tense when referring to John. You've only spoken about John in the present tense. That being said, we'll have to wait out the investigation to determine what the police believe."

Kate sat up. "Has anyone called John's mother?" she asked more to herself than to Doug or Michelle.

"I don't know," Doug answered, shaking his head. "They probably expect Bethany to notify her. Go get some sleep, if you can, and I'll give you a call tomorrow, OK?"

Kate nodded and walked Doug to the door. When she returned Michelle was on her phone texting furiously.

"Who are you texting at this hour?" Kate asked as she sat and pulled over her wine glass.

"I'm posting all of this to Facebook. You know people are wondering why there were a bunch of cop cars in front of your house. What's the emoticon for a big steaming pile of shit?" Michelle asked.

Kate drained her wine glass then set it down in front of her and wondered if she had another bottle in the pantry. Michelle slid her half-full glass over to Kate.

"Thank you for being here," Kate said as she accepted the glass. "I don't know if I could have handled that on my own."

"Well, don't think I'm leaving," Michelle answered. "Try and get some rest. I'll stay down here on the couch in case anything else comes up."

Kate didn't have the energy to protest so she simply nodded and gave her friend a hug before going upstairs to call John's mother, Betty. She didn't notice the patrol car parked outside the house.

John's mother was surprisingly calm when Kate broke the news of John's death. She hung up, saddened and confused by the other woman's seeming lack of concern. She knew if she'd lost Emma or Lizzie, she would be devastated. And even though she and John had divorced under terrible circumstances, Kate could feel her shock give way to a bitter ache in her heart knowing that he was no longer a part of the world. As bad a husband as he had been, he'd been a major part of her life for so long that she felt like a piece of her had died with him.

Kate lay back and closed her eyes and tried to process her very complicated feelings.

The next day, the news had taken the story of John's murder and reported it on an endless loop. Kate sent the girls upstairs hoping to shield them from the horror of what had really happened to their father. She and Michelle watched until they couldn't take it anymore. She had just turned the TV off when Doug came by in the early afternoon. With his connections to law enforcement, he was able to get a great deal of information about the investigation. Michelle took his visit as an opportunity to run home to take a shower.

Lizzie and Emma were playing in their rooms when he stepped into the foyer.

"How are you doing?"

Kate gave him a look that wasn't quite a smile. "It's been rough," she admitted.

"And how are they doing?" he asked, nodding up the stairs. Kate shrugged.

"I told them someone hurt daddy really badly and that his body couldn't work anymore, so he went to heaven to be with the angels," she said quietly.

"And how did they take that?" he asked.

This time Kate smiled but sadly. "Well, they're doubting the heaven part, but they understood the rest. They're sad, but he'd been really hard on them. They think he's being punished for being a bad daddy. Emma's especially bothered by that idea. One of our priests is coming over tomorrow to work with them."

"Good...that's good," Doug looked satisfied at the news. "Let's sit down."

Kate led him into the family room.

"So, one of the guys assigned to John's murder is a good friend of mine and gave me a rundown on where they are so far. Apparently, John suffered more than ten penetrating stab wounds to the throat and upper torso. Post mortem won't be complete for a few days, but they're pretty sure with the amount of blood on the scene, that one of the stab wounds nicked his carotid artery, and he bled to death." Doug stopped as Kate's face went pale. "You want me to go on or do you want to stop?"

Kate shook her head, though she wasn't certain she could handle any more.

Doug took that as a yes and continued. "So, Bethany Stephens claims she found him around nine o'clock yesterday morning when she returned home after staying with a girlfriend, and early post mortem indicates he died some time late the night before or early morning. He was nude, and blood trails and spatter suggest he was in bed when he was first stabbed, then tried to crawl toward the door where he died on the floor." Kate shuddered so Doug stopped for a moment.

"That's the end of that part, at least for now, OK?" he asked gently. Kate nodded and gestured for him to continue.

"The condo is a mess. Crap everywhere like no one ever cleaned. They searched through it all and no weapon was recovered at the scene. Fingerprint dusting found only John and Bethany's prints in the bedroom and main part of the condo with two sets of smaller prints, probably the girls, in the living room and one of the bedrooms. They pulled your fingerprint file from the state's records you submitted when you got your licensing and found that your prints were in the condo as well but only in the girls' bedroom."

Kate looked confused. "How could my fingerprints be there if *I've* never been there?" she asked.

Doug looked at his notes. "They were found on a picture frame, some toys, and a handful of books," he said by way of an answer.

"Oh. I gave those to John so the girls would have something familiar in his house."

"Otherwise, there's no other trace evidence that you or anyone else was there," he continued. "But Bethany Stephens is insistent that you're either the killer, or you were involved."

Kate looked indignant. "That's bullshit. I have nothing to gain from John's death. The custody modification was rejected, and with John dead there's no child support anymore. We're already divorced, and I'm glad we are. These last two months I've wondered how we stayed married in the first place. We even changed our life insurance policies."

Doug glanced down at his notebook. "That doesn't seem to be the case as far as the investigators have determined. How were they changed?" he asked.

Kate looked confused. "Under the terms of the divorce we were to remove each other's name as beneficiary and assign a family member as financial guardian for the girls. Since I don't have any family, if I die, my assets, including my life insurance benefit, would go into a trust until they turn twenty-one. John's mother is financial guardian for his policy."

Doug shook his head. "Nope. Apparently, he never changed it."

"Why does that matter?" she asked. "The policies didn't hold much value anyway. I think mine is somewhere around $50,000, and his is $100,000."

Doug shook his head again. "Nope again. John's policy has a benefit of $1,000,000 and with his double indemnity clause, payout is $2,000,000."

Kate was surprised but still shrugged. "That still doesn't have anything to do with me. The girls are his beneficiaries, not me. I can't touch a dime of his life insurance money and neither can they until they're legal adults."

Doug raised his eyebrows. "John increased his policy at the end of June and kept you specifically as the beneficiary. He also had a policy through his dental practice that names the girls as beneficiaries."

This time Kate was shocked. "Are you sure?" she asked. Doug nodded.

"Are *you* sure you didn't know anything about it?" he asked.

"Positive. I'd already changed my policy by then. Why wouldn't he do the same?" she asked.

"I'm not sure we'll ever find out," Doug answered. "Did you know that you're listed as the owner of the policy?"

This time Kate nodded. "I was his, and he was mine. That way, the payout is exempt from estate taxes."

Doug looked impressed. "Interesting. But I've got one more important thing I need to talk to you about. Apparently, they found a shirt at the scene. It had blood spatters and a blood handprint on it consistent with his attacker wearing it. Bethany insists that it's your shirt."

Kate shook her head. "I don't know why she would think that...oh my God." Kate's face went pale again. "Lizzie took one of my shirts to wear to bed the last time they were there."

"Do you know if she brought it home with her?" he asked.

"I didn't open their bags yet," she answered. "Let me check."

Kate ran upstairs and went into Lizzie's room. She could hear the girls playing in Emma's room, so as quietly as possible, she zipped open Lizzie's bag and pulled everything out before heading back downstairs.

"It's not here."

Doug's lips pressed into a thin grim line. "Then I'm going to have to talk to Lizzie at some point and so will the investigators," he said. "Are you going to be OK with that?"

Kate nodded slowly. "If I can't be there, I want either the GAL or our priest there with her."

"I agree," Doug replied. "Now, they're also going to want you to submit a DNA sample, and I suggest you comply."

"I will," Kate insisted.

"And as far as timing goes, the view from the security cameras on Jeff's house include most of your driveway so we can pull his DVR record to prove that you didn't drive away, at least."

"I didn't do this. Why do I have to work so hard to prove that?" Kate asked.

"With no witnesses or confession, the investigators are going to have to build their case on motive, access, and whatever circumstantial evidence they can find. We need to anticipate what they might find and what they might try to use against you."

"But why me? Bethany has more of a reason to kill him than I do." Kate said.

Doug shook his head. "Not really. John's attorney says he never changed his will and he didn't take you off his life insurance. In fact, he increased it considerably and kept you as beneficiary. Between that and the value of his assets and his practice, you stand to benefit the most from John's death...not her, and don't think the police don't already know that."

"Are they at least investigating her?" Kate asked.

"They're probably not looking at her as closely but they have to rule her out completely in order to build a case against you."

"Unbelievable," Kate said. "So, I could go to prison anyway? Even dead, John's screwing me over."

Doug looked sympathetic. "I'll make sure that doesn't happen. Now, would it be OK if I talk to Lizzie and Emma?"

Kate nodded. "I'll go get them."

The girls were playing quietly with their dolls when Kate opened Emma's door. "Hey, Mr. Doug from down the street wants to say hi. Is that OK?"

Emma looked up. "He wants to ask about Daddy, doesn't he?"

Kate sank in front of her and pulled Emma into her arms. "Yes, baby, is that OK?"

Emma nodded against her mother's neck, then pulled away and held her hand out to her sister. "Come on, Lizzie." Kate watched with great sadness as Lizzie silently pushed off the floor and took her sister's hand. Together they made their way down the stairs.

Kate fell against Emma's bed and let the tears fall.

After a long day of visits from Doug and Michelle and phone calls from everyone else, Kate was grateful to shut everything down and let the quiet fall over her. She hadn't taken a moment yet to fully process what was going on and she really needed to work through both her feelings and the profound change in circumstances to her life.

She had put the girls to bed earlier but was unable to sleep so she moved over to the overstuffed armchair in her bedroom and sat staring out the window, when she heard a quiet cry.

Kate jumped up and looked in Lizzie's room first and saw that she was still sleeping. She moved to Emma's room.

"Mom?"

Kate pushed open the door and poked her head in.

"Emma?" she asked. "Are you OK?"

"Can you come sit with me?" Emma asked in a small voice.

Kate moved into the room and sat next to where Emma lay on her bed.

"What's up, buttercup? Did you have a bad dream?"

Emma shook her head. "I can't fall asleep."

Kate reached over and ran her fingers through Emma's soft brown hair. Emma turned her head and pressed her face into Kate's hand. Kate could feel tears against her palm.

"Oh, sweetheart," Kate crooned. "What's wrong?"

"Are you going to die?" Emma asked with a hitch in her voice.

"No, sweetheart," Kate answered. "Not for a very long time."

"But Daddy's dead now," Emma said. Kate understood the depth of Emma's fear beneath the unfinished statement. She knew that in her daughter's unspoken words lay the logic that if one parent could be taken away, so could another.

"What happened to daddy was unique...rare...and it won't happen again...at least not to us."

Even in the dark, Emma looked doubtful. Kate leaned over and gathered Emma into her arms and held her close as Emma's sobs shook her small body.

SIXTEEN

Kate asked Annabelle to stay with the girls then spent the morning at the police station giving her statement and submitting a DNA sample.

To their credit, the investigators acted impartial and their questions were no different than the ones Doug had already asked.

By the time Kate got home the front page of the local newspaper had already covered the story of John's murder. Her photo was lined up with John and Bethany's photos. Of the three, hers was the most flattering. John's photo was an old one from a brochure he'd used in previous years until a patient told him it made his face look fat and Bethany's looked like her high school graduation photo that highlighted some questionable style choices. Kate skimmed the article but it didn't have anything in it she didn't already know, and she was glad nothing had been sensationalized. It was actually pretty benign. Still, she threw it in the recycling bin so the girls wouldn't see it by accident.

Lizzie and Emma came running as she opened the door. Annabelle wasn't far behind. Kate could hear the phone ringing in the other room.

She gave Annabelle a quizzical look as she gave the girls hugs.

"Yeah, it's been doing that all morning. I answered the first few, but it's been nothing but reporters and a couple of nut jobs, so I let the rest go to voicemail. It's all over the news too so we just kept the TV off."

"Oh Annabelle, I'm so sorry," Kate said. "I didn't even think about that."

"No worries," Annabelle smiled. "Do you want me to stay?"

Kate shook her head. "Thanks, but I think I'm going to unplug the phone and let the girls have some quiet time."

"OK." She bent down to give the girls hugs. "I'll see you guys later."

Lizzie and Emma returned her hug enthusiastically and waved as Annabelle left.

Kate went into the kitchen and unplugged the phone when the doorbell rang. Afraid that it was the press in person, she made the girls stay in the family room while she went to check.

Patrick stood there, his face a mask of sadness. "I hope it's OK, but I saw the news, and I was worried about you and the girls."

Lizzie and Emma caught sight of Patrick and came running to throw their arms around him. Kate was surprised to see Emma crying.

"Hey, big girl," Patrick crooned, as he held Emma close and stroked her hair. "It's going to be OK."

Emma pulled back and looked at him, her face red and wet with tears. "You can't go away again, OK? I don't want you to leave us."

Patrick gave her a big hug. "I'm not, Em. I'm not going anywhere." He looked at Kate. "Right?" he asked.

Holding back her own tears, Kate nodded.

Patrick was true to his word and stuck close to Kate and the girls. With the increase in scrutiny, it was inevitable that their relationship would be made public and Doug was less than pleased. He said as much during their next meeting.

"So, when were you going to tell me about the boyfriend?" he asked, when Kate let him in a few days later.

"I'm so sorry. We weren't seeing each other when John died and I didn't even think to mention it."

Doug frowned as he sat down at the table. "I'm going to need to speak with him, and I can guarantee the police are going to look closely at him."

"That's fine," Patrick said from the doorway. "I'll talk to whoever you want me to."

Doug stood, and Patrick crossed the room to shake his hand. "I'm Patrick, by the way. You're Doug, right?"

Doug nodded and sat down again. "I have a couple of things to discuss with you. There've been some developments."

Kate felt her stomach clench. From Doug's tone, developments sounded like a bad thing.

"Which do you want first? Good news or bad news?"

"Bad news," Kate answered.

"Bethany Stephens has accused you of sending threatening emails and text messages to both her and John. They look anonymous, but the email looks like it could be yours, and the content suggests information that only you and they would know."

Kate was dumbstruck. "I've never sent anything to either of them. John and I didn't communicate by email, and I don't even know hers. And John's the one who's been sending *me* text messages. I don't even answer them. I just delete them."

Doug didn't answer but pushed a pile of printouts toward her. Kate pulled them closer and started to read. Patrick read them over her shoulder.

There were so many that Kate couldn't even read them all, but from what she could see, every single one of them was filled with bile spewing vitriol.

"*You think you can still my man and take all my shit and I'm just gonna let you well you can just think agin.*" Kate read aloud then shook her head. "I didn't write these."

Doug looked at her closely. "Are you sure? People don't always sound like themselves when they're angry."

Kate pushed them back to Doug and pointed to the one on top. "First, crichrson@live.com isn't my email, and even if I'd made it up, I would have at least spelled my own name correctly. And there are so many expletives and misspellings in the text, it reads like an angry middle-schooler wrote it. If I'd written these they'd at least be grammatically correct."

Doug pulled them back over and read the one she'd chosen. "They'll want to look at your computer and they'll definitely pull your phone records," he warned. "Will they find anything?"

"There isn't anything to find," Kate said. "They're welcome to it."

Doug nodded and made a note of that. "Then you can surrender it voluntarily. That'll look good to them. What do you use here? A laptop?"

"Yes. I don't use it for much." She retrieved her computer from the office and placed it in front of him. "Now, what's the good news?"

Doug flipped the pages in his notebook. "It's really two things, or three, depending on how you look at it. First, the post mortem is done and they are releasing John's body soon. Second, there's a security camera in the parking lot at Amber Woods that faces the stairs that leads to John's condo, and according to the video from around the time of John's murder, you were not there. It's hard to tell because the image quality is not that great but only a handful of people are seen coming and going from the building, and none of them look like you."

Kate sighed with relief. "Finally something that backs me up. Wait, what's the third thing?"

Doug smiled. "This is a good one. We found out from John's mother why he never changed the beneficiary designation on his life insurance policy. Apparently, Bethany suggested he increase his policy and since they were supposed to be having a baby together, either she or the baby would need to be named as beneficiary. When John discussed the change with his mother, he mentioned that he was nervous about Bethany getting involved in his financial business, so his mother suggested keeping you the sole beneficiary so Emma and Lizzie would be taken care of."

"But why wouldn't he keep Betty as their fiduciary?" Kate was confused.

"I asked her that and she said with her health issues, she knew you'd outlive her. She also said that she felt like you would take care of things appropriately and John agreed because he knew that no matter what happened to him, you would put the girls first. He expressed doubts about Bethany and her pregnancy and Betty is prepared to testify to that. She's flying in to take care of his funeral arrangements, by the way. The coroner will release John's body to her when she arrives."

Kate sat back. "I'm glad John was thinking about the girls for once."

Doug held up a hand. "Before you go putting a halo on him, the guy got himself involved with a woman while he was still married to you then left to move in with her. That doesn't exactly make him father of the year."

"I told him to leave. And he did love his girls. He may not have been great at showing it but he wasn't a terrible father."

"OK, half a halo then," Doug conceded then turned his attention to Patrick, who had taken a seat next to Kate. "I'm going to get to you in a second," he warned. Doug was about to continue when his cell phone went off. He jumped up. "I've got to take this," he said, then stepped out onto the deck.

Patrick took Kate's hand and looked at her sympathetically. "You OK?" he asked.

Kate smiled. "I'm fine. Just tired." The two sat quietly as Doug paced the length of the deck with his phone to his ear.

"I wonder if I should be worried," Kate remarked. Patrick squeezed her hand.

"I don't know. He doesn't look happy."

Sure enough, Doug was frowning when he stepped back in.

"They want to talk to you again but they're not telling me why."

"Am I still a suspect?" Kate asked, shocked that she even had to ask such a question.

"Everyone's a suspect unless they completely eliminated. I'm going to assume they've found some kind of hole in your alibi for that night."

"So if Kate can't prove she was here all night that makes her guilty?" Patrick asked.

Doug shook his head. "Not exactly. Lack of an alibi doesn't automatically indicate guilt; it just means they're looking at her more closely than before. We still need to cooperate with their requests but we'll hope it just an effort to eliminate you as a suspect."

"Isn't that what they were doing before?" Patrick asked. "Eliminating Kate as a suspect?"

Doug frowned. "It's a little more subtle than that. With no confession or witnesses, investigators will use the evidence available and approach suspects as either someone to eliminate or someone to build a case around. Since multiple stabbings are very personal in nature, they're going to look at someone who knew him well, had access and means to commit the murder, and had a compelling reason to want him dead. And then there's the number of stab wounds." Doug checked his notes. "Coroner found eighteen points of entry, all but two fully penetrating. It takes a lot of anger to stab someone that deep that many times, so they're going to focus on who was angry enough for that much overkill. That leaves Kate as their primary candidate, then Bethany."

"That sucks," Patrick stated. Doug agreed.

"And that's why defense attorneys exist. With enough circumstantial evidence, police and prosecutors can send innocent people to prison for a very long time. I want to avoid that."

Kate let go of Patrick's hand and took Doug's. "And I want to thank you for that. I can't tell you how much I appreciate your helping me like this."

Doug smiled. "You're welcome. Now let's keep up the momentum and surrender your laptop, so they have more to pin on Bethany. Can you find someone to stay with the girls?"

"I can stay with them," Patrick offered. "I'll take them outside to play."

Doug nodded, and he and Kate stood up. Doug reached over to shake Patrick's hand. "Take good care of them," he said sternly then smiled. "They need a lot of love right now."

Kate gave Patrick a hug and left with Doug.

SEVENTEEN

By the time she got home, Kate was emotionally exhausted. Patrick needed to get to work so she gave him a kiss and thanked him for staying with the girls. When she mentioned the funeral, she tried not to be hurt by his request to be excused from attending. She wanted to understand his feelings but it still bothered her that he actively didn't want to be there to support her. It seemed so much like something John would do. Kate kept the emotion out of her voice and told him it was OK then tried not to take offense when he looked relieved. After he left, Kate called John's mother, Betty, and found out that she was flying in from Ohio the next afternoon. Kate offered to pick her up at the airport. Betty accepted.

Kate and the girls had a quiet evening as a family. The next morning they set off for the airport. Lizzie and Emma were happy to see their nana. Betty had graciously avoided taking sides in the divorce but Kate was still nervous about seeing her.

They found a spot in the short-term parking lot and went in to wait for Betty in the arrivals terminal. Kate was surprised to see Betty brought out in a wheelchair and worried that the older woman's health was worse than she had originally thought. But Betty's smile was huge as she held out her arms to the girls.

"There are my beautiful grandbabies!" she cried. "Come give Grandma big hugs!"

Lizzie threw her arms around Betty's neck, while a more somber Emma leaned into her and let Betty hug her. When the girls moved away, Betty put her arms out to Kate who gratefully stepped over and hugged John's mother. She had been quietly dreading this encounter, worried that Betty would blame Kate for his infidelity, for the divorce... for everything really.

Both women were teary when Kate stepped back.

"Can we take the wheelchair with us to the car, or do we have to leave it here?" Kate asked the skycap who'd been pushing her ex-mother-in-law.

Betty answered for him. "This is my chair, hon. I'm not walking very well these days."

Kate was surprised. "Well thank you, then," she said to the gentleman who tipped his cap and set off to help another airport patron. "Do you have luggage we need to wait for?"

Betty patted at a spot over her shoulder. "It's strapped onto the back of my chair with my walker. We can just go."

When they got back to the house, Kate settled Betty into the family room and fed everyone an early dinner. The girls finished quickly and ran downstairs to play while Kate entertained the awkward conversation that was certain to come.

"I was wondering if you wanted to stay here with us instead of at a hotel. I moved the guest room down here so you won't have to try to navigate the stairs," Kate said as a conversation opener. "Is that OK?"

Betty gave her a smile of gratitude. "That would be lovely. I was worried I might need some help with the bathtub if I stayed somewhere else, but I didn't want to assume it would be OK to stay here. You've already done far more than any other ex-daughter-in-law would," she answered. "I imagine this isn't easy for you." Betty's expression was sympathetic.

Kate was grateful. "I just didn't know what to expect. John's your son. Of course you want to support him."

Betty sniffed and Kate could see her eyes fill with tears. "John was an ass for what he did. I don't know what he was thinking taking up with that girl."

"Have you met her?" Kate asked. It had never occurred to her that John would introduce Bethany to his mother, but then she wondered why he wouldn't when Bethany was supposedly pregnant.

Betty took a prim sip of her iced tea. "He brought her to meet me just before the divorce," she answered. "I was not impressed. The girl can barely string two sentences together and spent most of their visit in bed watching that stupid Kardashian family's TV show. Claiming she was having complications from the pregnancy, pthhhht." Betty's tone was dismissive. "She didn't seem to have any problems when John took her to the mall to go shopping. I doubt she was even really pregnant. I never saw her throw up once though she made a big show of finding everything I made for them nauseating. She hasn't contacted me once since John's passing. I never would have known he'd died if you hadn't called me." Betty sat shaking her head.

"She either lost the baby or...," Kate said delicately.

"Or she tricked John by faking a pregnancy? Poor John." Betty wiped her eyes with a napkin. "I can't believe he's gone. No parent should outlive their child. And who's going to take care of you now? I mean I know there's insurance and everything but the girls don't have a father anymore. My poor babies."

Kate didn't want to discuss the quality of John's parenting so she changed the subject.

"Can I ask why you had John make me the beneficiary?" Kate asked. "It was part of the divorce settlement that you serve as financial guardian for the girls."

"Oh, honey," Betty lamented. "Just look at me. My health is so awful I can barely manage my own affairs. Those girls deserve better than what I can do for them," she answered. "Despite everything that's happened, to me you're still my son's wife and my grandbabies' mother. I trust you, and I think John trusted you too."

Kate was touched.

"Are you comfortable going with me to the funeral home?" Betty asked. Kate nodded. "Good, I don't want that girl anywhere near me or my son. Now if you don't mind, I'd like to rest awhile."

Kate jumped up. "Of course, let me help you." She wheeled Betty into the bedroom and steadied her while she moved from her chair to the bed.

Betty slept until the next morning. Once the girls got off to school, Kate helped her with her shower and dressing so the two could attend to John's funeral arrangements.

The funeral director had his hands full with Betty. She was determined to keep John's memorial service as small and inexpensive as possible. Kate was surprised that Betty did not want a traditional funeral service for her son, but figured since it was her son she could do whatever she wanted. She still felt like she should offer though.

"Are you sure you don't want to have it at St. John's?" Kate asked. "I know they would accommodate you even though John wasn't a parishioner."

"No, dear," Betty answered. "If he had been a regular church-goer then I'd say yes, but it would be hypocritical to ask them to host his funeral. John never gave faith much credence."

"Do you have a funeral notice prepared or would you like us to put one together for you?" the funeral director asked.

Kate and Betty both stared at him blankly. "Funeral notice for what?" Betty asked.

"For the newspaper," he answered. "I'm sure you want people to know when to come."

Betty was shaking her head even before he'd finished his sentence. "This is a private service. I don't want a viewing and I'm not printing an open invitation in the newspaper so that any Tom, Dick, and Harry can show up and gawk at us. Family only and my family has already been notified. If Kate wants to extend an invitation to John's staff, then that's up to her," she stated firmly.

"Just Barb, his practice manager," Kate answered. "She's been with him since the beginning and she's a very nice lady. She would want to be there, so...I can call her."

Betty gave a short nod. "That's it, then," she said. "No more."

The funeral director looked like he wanted to protest but wisely kept his opinion to himself. "As you wish. Everything is in order for Friday then. The memorial will begin at ten o'clock and you may have a small private remembrance at the cremation."

"I still think we should just do a direct cremation," she sniffed. Betty pulled out her checkbook. "Then we don't even need to rent the coffin."

"I think people would think it was suspicious," Kate said gently. "I know you're angry with him, but there are others who would like to say goodbye."

"He's dead," Betty grumbled. "It's not like he's even going to know."

Kate wanted to smile but didn't. John had inherited his mother's agnostic leanings, which obviously extended to the absence of any type of afterlife. Luckily, Betty didn't begrudge Kate her desire to live a more spiritual life the way her son had.

"These things are always for the living," Kate replied. "It'll give them closure."

Betty sighed but gave in.

They signed the rest of the paperwork, and Betty handed over the check. Kate had offered to pay for the funeral costs, but Betty waved the offer away.

"We have several options for the cremation remains." The director pushed a brochure across the desk. "We have many very lovely urns and can even have his ashes made into a diamond if you wish, or a cremation pendant. Our jewelry selection is high quality silver, white gold, and gold, and we can divide the remains to fashion memorial necklaces for as many members of the family as you wish."

Kate stifled a cough as Betty looked at him in horror. "Is this some kind of a joke?" she asked, indignant. "Why on earth would I want to *wear* my dead son? That's the most disgusting thing I..."

Kate spared the young man from further humiliation and pulled the urn brochure over. She tapped on a black marble urn while Betty continued her rant.

"This will be fine," she said. The young man smiled gratefully.

"How about I just bill you," he offered and Kate agreed. The quicker they wrapped this up, the better.

Kate thanked him and pushed Betty out of the office.

"Who on earth wants to wear a dead person? Have you ever heard of anything more morbid? Good grief."

The drive home was mercifully short. Betty was still indignant about the idea of wearing her son's ashes so she settled into the guest room to calm down while Kate fetched Lizzie from the bus stop.

By the time dinner rolled around, Betty was calm again. After dinner, Kate helped Emma with her homework and sent the girls to their rooms for quiet time before bed. Betty used Kate's laptop to email family about the time and location of the memorial service. She was done quickly and Kate wondered how many people were actually going to show up. Though John's practice was in Maryland, his family all lived in Ohio where he grew up and went to college. He'd gone to dental school in Maryland then worked with a local practice before taking it over from his boss when he retired. Though he boasted many cousins, John's parents had divorced long ago when his father left the family, and he only had two other siblings, Daniel, who'd died years ago and Joanna, a sister with profound emotional issues that had resulted in multiple stays in various psychiatric facilities and rehab centers. Betty had finally hit her limit with the girl and kicked her out of her house. Kate was pretty sure from the few phone calls John had received from his sister in the last few months they'd lived together that Jo was homeless.

Kate looked at Betty more closely. Her former mother-in-law looked extremely tired and she'd clearly been crying again. Kate felt guilty that she hadn't shed more tears for the man she'd shared part of her life with.

"Are you feeling OK?" she asked, accidently startling the older woman.

Even Betty's smile was tired. "I don't have the energy I used to. Days like this tend to wear me out faster than they did before."

Kate tried to be tactful. "Can I ask what's wrong...medically?"

"I have leukemia," Betty answered. "Acute Myeloid Leukemia to be exact."

"Oh my goodness." Kate was shocked. "John never said anything. When did you find out?"

"Earlier this year," she answered. "I was feeling extremely tired all the time and kept having hot flashes like I was going through menopause again. Then the bruising started. My primary misdiagnosed it as hormonal at first, but my GYN suspected anemia and sent me to an oncologist for a bone marrow test. Really, the chemo is worse than the leukemia." Betty put her hand up to her forehead and self-consciously touched the short fine hair surrounding her face. "I just got my hair back."

"When do you find out if the chemo was successful?" Kate asked.

Betty sighed. "It wasn't. I've already had my follow-up. I'm thinking about seeing someone at Hopkins at some point, but I don't want to impose on you any more than I already have."

"It's no imposition," Kate insisted. "I'll take you to Hopkins myself. In fact, I wanted to ask you if you'd like to stay here with us for an extended visit. The girls love having you here, and if it means you have access to better care, then there's no reason for you not to stay."

Betty seemed to consider Kate's offer. "I don't want to be a burden to you," she said carefully. "Especially if I have to go through another round of chemo."

"It's not a burden, Betty," Kate said sincerely. "You're Lizzie and Emma's only grandparent. I'd like to keep you around as long as possible."

Betty smiled at Kate's generosity. "I'd have to find someone to help take care of my sister, Patty."

"Is she ill too?" Kate was surprised. Betty's older sister had always been full of health and vigor.

"She had a stroke last year," Betty said. "She can get around a little bit, but she can't talk, and she can't feed or toilet herself."

"And you've been caring for her...even with the leukemia?" Kate asked. "What about her children?"

Betty sniffed. "They help out when they can, but they're not very reliable. But I can figure something out when I go back after the funeral."

"Let me know how I can help," Kate said.

"Thank you. Just offering is far more than John can do now." Betty sounded angry.

"I understand you're angry with John," she began delicately. "Would you like to talk about it?"

Betty's smile was rueful. "Are you counseling me?" she asked, but it was not a challenge.

Kate smiled back. "Maybe," she answered. "I'm not going to psycho-analyze you if that's what you're worried about. I just thought it might help you to talk about how you're feeling with someone who under-stands your relationship with John firsthand."

Betty sighed. "I'm just so furious with him. When he told me he got that Bethany girl pregnant...I'll admit I wasn't surprised. His father was just as faithless. But I was so disappointed. I thought he'd learned from his father's abandonment the damage that kind of behavior could cause. But he turned out selfish. I just can't understand how he could do something so awful to his own family."

"Children often model their same sex parent," Kate said. "Unless they make a concerted effort to break the pattern of behavior, they will unconsciously follow that pattern to the same or similar conclusions."

"I thought John would have been smarter than that. He was cer-tainly smart enough to do well in college to go on to dental school. But, with all the time I've been spending with the oncologists, I've come to realize that they are all a bit full of themselves, aren't they?"

"Some do seem to take themselves very seriously," Kate admitted. "When we married, John still had a sense of faith in, if not God, then at least a creator. That changed over time, and when he died, he was a staunch and vocal atheist."

Betty looked embarrassed. "I should probably take the blame for that," she said. "My parents were strict evangelicals and I swore I would not raise my children with such a judgmental and narrow view of the world. Now they have nothing. And it's too late for John."

Betty started to cry. Kate held her mother-in-law's hand, while the other woman cried out the grief that had been held at bay by her anger.

"I made so many mistakes," Betty said through her tears. "I thought I would raise strong children...that they would be able to stand on their own two feet and build honest, noble lives. I gave them an excellent education thinking that was all they really needed to make the best choices for themselves. But I was too hard on them. My parents were not loving people and even though I tried to be a different kind of mother, I ended up making the same mistakes. John grew up petty and manipulative and his sister grew up weak and irresponsible. Poor Daniel didn't grow up at all."

"John had his bad side," Kate admitted. "But he took his responsibility to the girls very seriously. And Jo is dealing with her own demons. And she's still young...What is she, twenty-five? She has time to turn her life around."

Betty was done crying. She snorted as she wiped her eyes with her napkin. "Not saddled with a child she doesn't. And a special needs one at that."

Kate didn't know very much about John's sister, Jo. She was ten years younger than John and had only called her brother when she needed money.

"What do you mean by special needs?" Kate asked.

Betty sniffed. "She got pregnant during her bad time when she was into all the drugs and devil music or whatever. I haven't seen them in a long time but she told me Danny barely speaks even though he's seven or eight-years-old now. Apparently, he suffers from seizures. Not that she's taken him to a doctor or anything. I'm pretty sure they're living in a shelter up near Toledo or Akron. She won't tell me where they are."

"She named him after your youngest?" Kate asked.

Betty look annoyed. "Can you believe she did that? My baby boy goes missing when she's supposed to be babysitting him, and she names her son after him? Lord help me if she has another son and names him John. I feel like Job waiting for the other shoe to drop."

Kate smiled at the mixed idioms.

Betty caught the smile and laughed at her mistake. "Thank you, Kate. I appreciate what you're trying to do...and I appreciate your offer to stay here with you and the girls. Once I've figured out what to do about Patty, I'm going to take you up on your offer. I'm not even sixty yet. There's got to be something they can do."

EIGHTEEN

By the time Friday came around, Kate was already dreading the funeral. She was glad Patrick had begged off attending. Somehow the press got wind that John's memorial service had been scheduled and it was featured on the news like it was a state funeral. Betty was furious.

"I explicitly said I wanted a *private* service," she ranted. "Now everyone and their goddamned brother is going to be there."

Kate didn't answer and instead steered the girls to the backseat of the car before Betty could say more. Betty was still fussing when Kate came back to help her.

"And who thought it was their business to advertise it?" Kate shook her head but remained silent as she steadied her mother-in-law before lowering her into the passenger's seat. "I swear...if I find out, I'm going to...well, I don't know what I'm going to do, but I can guarantee you it won't be pretty."

Kate had no doubt about that.

When they arrived at the funeral home, Kate was surprised to see the parking lot half-full though it was still early. She'd figured on a packed house and was dreading having to explain to well-wishers that the cremation service itself was closed to the public. She already had her hands full with a mother-in-law who wasn't independently mobile and two girls who were terrified to go in and see their daddy even though Kate had reassured them that it was just a box and their daddy was already in heaven.

As they made their way inside, the funeral director came forward to greet them and guided them to the family section of the room that had been reserved for John's service. John's coffin already sat at the front of the room with his fat face portrait on an easel next to it. There was a surprising lack of flowers. Only a handful of bouquets accompanied the casket cover Kate had ordered for John's coffin.

Kate helped Betty transfer from her wheelchair to the pew then took a seat next to her with Lizzie and Emma seated on her other side. Michelle, her family, and Doug and his wife, Christine, weren't far behind. They took seats right behind Kate and Betty. She was surprised to see some unfamiliar faces and wondered if they were press, John's professional acquaintances, or the police. She didn't see any of John's extended family.

Kate looked around and saw there were a few neighborhood families among the mourners. Barb, John's practice manager, and her husband, Phil, were seated in the front row opposite them. Barb looked like she was taking John's death hard. Kate stood up and went over to give Barb a hug. Barb clutched Kate to her, her tears staining Kate's suit.

"I'm so sorry, Kate," Barb whispered. Kate patted Barb's back and murmured words of comfort in the other woman's ear then pulled away.

"Thank you for coming," Kate said. "John respected you so much. You made his life so much easier and I want you to know how much he valued you."

Barb smiled through her tears. "That is so kind of you. He never said anything but I always knew he appreciated everything I did for him." Barb reached over and hugged Kate again. Behind her, Kate saw Barb's husband looking away, his expression grim and slightly disgusted. She could tell he didn't share his wife's blind devotion to her employer. Kate returned Barb's hug. She took her seat next to Betty just as the funeral director began the service.

Betty had insisted on the shortest service possible and the director did not disappoint. He gave a brief welcome and eulogy and spoke as though he and John had been lifelong friends despite their never having met. Lizzie and Emma looked at him in confusion when they realized who he was talking about, and Kate could see Lizzie blinking back tears.

She pulled Lizzie over and had just placed her on her lap when she heard a commotion at the entrance. She turned in time to see Bethany and a woman who could only be her mother forcing their way in then marching up the center aisle to take a seat next to Barb and Phil.

"You have got to be kidding me," Betty said under her breath.

Barb looked noticeably discomfited, though to her credit Bethany looked beside herself with grief. Her mother was a slightly older, slightly pudgier twin and both were inappropriately dressed in tight black dresses and heels.

Betty gestured for the funeral director to come over.

"Yes, Mrs. Richardson? Is there a problem?" he asked, his tone anxious and conciliatory.

"What is that woman doing here?" she demanded. "I gave specific instructions that this was to be a private service."

The funeral director glanced at Bethany and looked back at Betty. "I'm sorry, but Dr. Richardson's fiancé contacted us regarding the schedule. I thought it was appropriate that she know what time to be here. She made it quite clear that you expected her to attend."

"I want her removed immediately," Betty ordered. Doug stood and moved to stand near them. Kate could see him nodding to one of the suited men seated nearby.

"Mrs. Richardson, you can't expect me to ask Miss Stephens to leave..." The funeral director put his hands up as if in surrender.

"That's exactly what I expect," Betty countered.

"You know, I can hear you," Bethany called out, her voice carrying over the crowd. Kate heard a collective gasp from the group behind them.

Betty pushed herself up off her seat, and Kate set Lizzie aside to help her. "Then you know you don't belong here," Betty said with impressive volume. "You have no business coming here and disrupting my son's funeral."

Bethany stood and moved closer to Betty, her mother right behind her. Bethany's face was swollen with tears and flushed red with anger.

"I belong here more than she does," Bethany said, nodding toward Kate. "They weren't even together anymore. He left her for me and she thinks she can tell me I can't be here to say goodbye? She has a boyfriend and now I don't have anyone." Everyone stared as the girl broke down sobbing.

Kate leapt forward and put herself between Bethany and Betty. "Please don't do this," she whispered. "My daughters lost their father and they don't need you making a scene in front of them."

Bethany wiped at her eyes smearing her mascara. "John didn't give a shit about those girls. He picked *me* and *not* you. He wanted to be *my* husband, not yours."

"You little piece of trash," Betty said, her voice low and threatening. "Don't you dare call my son your husband. He had no intention of marrying you. He knew exactly what you were...a whore. You think because you spread your legs like a whore, you deserve to get paid like one? Well, think again."

Bethany's mother feigned outrage and pushed her way in front of Betty. "You can't talk to my daughter like that."

Betty was about to respond when Doug and the suited gentlemen behind him moved between the mothers. Doug turned Betty aside as the others moved to escort Bethany and her mother out of the room.

"Hey, we don't have to leave. Tell *her* to leave," Bethany's mother called out, even as she was propelled toward the door. "My daughter has a right to say goodbye."

Kate didn't hear the rest. Lizzie and Emma had burst into tears. Kate sat between them and put her arms around them in an attempt to calm them down. Michelle took a seat on the other side of Emma and tried to help.

The funeral director moved back behind the lectern and started to resume the service when Betty loudly interrupted him.

"This *service* is finished," she announced to the room. "Thank you for coming. You may all go."

People looked at each other uncertainly. Some looked horrified at what had just taken place while others seemed to want to stay to help. Most began filing out, furiously whispering about what had just happened. Barb remained behind, her face beet red with tears and what looked like shame.

"I'm so sorry," she whispered to Kate. "I was the one that told her the service was today but I didn't tell her where. I didn't realize...I mean...I didn't know that she....God, I am so so sorry."

Kate wanted to tell her it was all right but Barb's husband stepped up at that moment and pulled his wife away.

"Good grief, what a shit show," Michelle muttered. Lizzie and Emma had calmed down enough for Kate to thank Doug for his help.

"Please accept my apologies, Mrs. Richardson," the funeral director said in a rush. "I had no idea."

"Just finish this quickly," she said quietly.

"Shall we proceed to the cremation service?" he asked. Kate looked at him, her expression incredulous.

"Just take care of it now," she answered. "We'll wait here."

The funeral director looked at the floor, clearly uncomfortable. "The actual cremation can take a while. Are you sure you want to wait?"

Kate took a deep breath. "No. We'll just leave now."

"Very good, ma'am," he answered with some of his composure returning. "I'll take care of everything else and call you to schedule a time to recover his remains."

"Fine."

"Can we go now?" Lizzie asked, her normal aplomb completely absent.

"Yes," Kate answered. "We can leave now."

"They know not to come to the house, don't they?" Betty asked as Doug helped her into her wheelchair.

Michelle snorted. "I can assure you no one from the neighborhood will be there after witnessing that."

Betty nodded. "Good. I'm tired and my flight's in a few hours. I'd like to rest before I leave."

Kate thanked everyone then took Betty and the girls home.

NINETEEN

It was with great relief that Kate dropped Betty off at the airport for her return flight to Ohio. After the disaster that was John's funeral, she needed some quiet time.

Several more days passed before anything happened. Kate kept waiting for some news of the investigation, but if the investigators were anything, they were methodical. The press was surprisingly mum as well and nothing had been in the paper since the first article.

Finally, Doug reported that Kate had unofficially been ruled out since little to no evidence existed to suggest that she had anything to do with John's death.

Despite her exoneration, things seemed to go from bad to worse for Kate. Patrick was in the midst of his final semester for his master's program and had taken a management position at another facility closer to campus, so Kate would only see him on occasional weekends unless things changed for him. He called or texted every day, which almost made it worse knowing that she couldn't physically look to him for comfort. She could hardly blame him for leaving. She'd inadvertently pulled him into her mess of a life and, though he stated otherwise, she knew it couldn't have been easy for him.

Worse, she'd been officially let go from a job she hadn't even started yet. The treatment center had called and rescinded their job offer citing budget issues but Kate knew better. Though she had some savings, money was getting extremely tight. Betty did her best but the insurance company continued to hold payment pending the outcome of the criminal investigation. Luckily, the court released John's assets and accounts and since John had kept Kate as his beneficiary for everything else, she was able to at least pay the mortgage on the house and buy food. She even had a buyer for his practice. The proceeds from its sale couldn't come fast enough.

The final blow came when the church called to invite her in to discuss the future of her role with the support group. Apparently, Linda had been actively campaigning behind her back and had finally worn them down. Reverend Jess tried to ease the sting by inviting Kate to start a new group for women who were widowed after divorce, though Kate secretly wondered if she could still be considered a widow. Since Evelyn's husband Harris had just died, she would be taking Evelyn with her. All that remained was to break it to the rest of the ladies.

Michelle took the girls for the night, so that Kate could host her final meeting. She left early to try to beat Linda so she could set up in peace but unfortunately Linda arrived shortly after her and was already gloating over her victory.

"Oh, finally," Linda chirped as if she'd been there the whole time despite walking in minutes behind Kate. "Were you running late? I should have given you my cell number so you could have let me know. We have a lot to discuss if I'm going to be successful at helping these ladies cope with their issues. You know, I've always had a lot of ideas that could have been of great benefit to whatever you were trying to accomplish..."

"Linda," Kate interrupted. "I sincerely want to wish you the best of luck in your effort to promote your ideas with this particular group of women. Count yourself successful if you manage to even get them to come back."

"Oh." Linda looked taken aback. "Thank you. You know, I told Reverend Jess that, given the mess you've found yourself in, it would be for the benefit of the group if you 'took a step back' as it were, to sort out your own affairs before you tried to help anyone else."

Kate stared at the other woman, amazed at her arrogance. "That's you Linda, always thinking about how you can do things better than someone else." She didn't bother to wait for Linda's response. She pushed past her to the meeting room where some of the other women were already getting their tea or coffee. Kate sat down and groaned inwardly when Linda sat down next to her. One silver lining was that she'd never have to see Linda ever again. She wasn't surprised when no one took the seat on the other side of her. Poor Judith was the last to arrive and her expression at finding that the only empty chair was next to Linda was priceless.

"Welcome Judith. I'm glad to see you here," Kate said. "Well ladies, I have some rather important news this evening. Evelyn's ex-husband passed away early this week so she will no longer be with us. Instead she'll be moving to a 'Widowed after Divorce' group."

"There's a support group for that?" Judith asked.

"Oh, yes," Kate answered as Linda nodded enthusiastically next to her. "You'll find there are as many support groups as there are problems."

Georgia leaned toward Judith and drawled, "Honey, if you were a one-eyed, one-horned, flying purple people eater with an anxiety disorder, you'd find a support group, no problem."

Kate let everyone have a laugh at that before continuing.

"All right, ladies, let's move on to our second bit of news," she said with a sigh. "I will be leaving as your facilitator and moving onto another group." This too was met with gasps and loud protestations. Kate felt flattered. "Now, now, that's not all," she continued. "Your new facilitator will be...Linda." There was nothing but stunned silence at this announcement as everyone's mouth fell open and Linda started preening.

"Well, that's a real kick in the head," Georgia said, finally breaking the silence.

Kate silently agreed. "Well, Linda feels she has a great deal to offer as a facilitator and...to be honest, her persistence has paid off. So, this will be my last meeting. Linda will take over next week."

"I promise to do my best," Linda said proudly.

Kate watched the glances pass among the women and knew none of them were going to be returning. "Let's make this a great night, OK?" she said, trying to sound positive. "The best one we've had yet."

Everyone nodded. Satisfied, Kate began the meeting.

Despite her silence at the beginning, Linda ended up monopolizing the conversation and it was with great relief when the time came to end the meeting. Kate led them through the Serenity Prayer, said her goodbyes then stepped out of the room so the ladies could work out what they wanted to do next. Unfortunately Linda followed her while the rest made a break for it.

"I'm going to need copies of all of your support materials," Linda said. "I don't suppose you kept a file."

Kate turned and faced Linda squarely. "You'll need to figure that one out on your own, Linda. The church will give you the newsletters and event schedules but I created everything else."

Linda sniffed. "Well I'd think you'd at least want them to have some sort of continuity. You certainly don't expect me to start from scratch, do you?"

"What you do with this group is not my problem anymore," Kate replied. "Besides, I have a feeling that you're going to have plenty of time to figure out how you want to run things. But, the first thing you'll need to do is clean up after the refreshments. That's your job now."

Kate didn't wait for an answer. She turned and left the building.

Now that the girls were in school, Kate had the mornings to herself until they came home. With nothing to do she needed something to occupy her time. She'd been active at the school when Emma started, and she didn't want Lizzie to feel cheated, so Kate signed up as a classroom volunteer during kindergarten orientation. Things seemed OK when she walked into the classroom on Lizzie's first day. Miss White, Lizzie's teacher, was warm and welcoming and deeply grateful for the help so Kate got right down to work setting out materials for their first craft.

Prior to the start of school, Kate had met with both the girls' teachers and the school psychologist about how best to support the girls during the investigation into their father's death and the subsequent publicity surrounding it. Though children their age were mostly immune to the world outside their own homes, their parents weren't, and the school wanted to forestall any fallout on the girls for as long as possible. Both teachers showed great restraint, though Kate could tell they were itching to ask her about the murder. The television and print news had been surprisingly circumspect with the story and little had been reported since the initial article.

In an effort to keep busy, Kate had accidently exhausted the supply of die cut leaves the children had been given to decorate then tape to the door of the kindergarten pod so she offered to cut more for the afternoon class. Miss White was grateful and handed her a ream of autumn colored construction paper. Kate made her way to the volunteer room where the die cut machine was located. Kate heard her name and stopped just outside the doorway. She couldn't tell how many moms were in there but Kate could clearly hear the women talking about her. Kate was hesitant to go in, as much out of curiosity as embarrassment to be the topic of conversation and at the school no less.

"I'm amazed she's even here," she heard one woman say. "She's had a patrol car in front of her house for the last few weeks. I wouldn't think she'd be allowed to come into the school."

"She didn't kill a kid," the other one joked. "Maybe they think she'll just stick to husbands. I feel bad for the girlfriend, having to find that? Yikes."

"Seriously," the first one continued. "I heard from Diane that there was blood everywhere and she'd stabbed him so many times his head was almost detached."

"And how could she possibly know that?" she heard a third voice ask. "The newspaper only said he was stabbed, nothing about being decapitated. You might want to wait until they actually arrest her before you start passing judgment." Kate was grateful that at least one person was standing up for her. "And if she did do it, who could blame her? He was kind of a dick."

"Oh my God, Mary! How can you say that? The man is dead!"

Kate realized her defender was Mary Morgan, a friend of Michelle's. She didn't know her well, but right now Kate loved Mary with all her heart.

"And that somehow makes him a saint now? Give me a break. The guy was an asshole. I don't mean to say that he deserved to die for being an asshole. I'm just saying I'm not surprised."

160

"I just don't think it's right to speak ill of the dead," the first one said. Kate could hear scorn in her voice.

"Just the living, right?" Mary's tone was sarcastic. "You might not feel that way if you'd ever heard him talk about the women in the neighborhood. Bill went golfing with him a couple of times and John had plenty of unflattering things to say about all of us, including your girlfriend Diane."

"What did he say about Diane?" Kate heard one of them ask.

"So much I can't even remember it all." Mary answered. "All I know is he had crappy nicknames for all of us."

"Not me," the second one protested. "I barely knew him."

"That didn't stop him from saying you were fat and stupid," Mary retorted, "which seemed to be his opinion of most of the women here. I feel sorry for Kate. No wonder she's so skinny. And before you go repeating what Diane says about people, you might want to ask her what she says about the two of you."

Kate smiled at that then startled when Mary left the volunteer room and ran straight into her. To her credit, Mary looked mortified at having been caught talking about her. Kate smiled and was about to reassure her when Mary spoke first.

"I'm really sorry about that....and about everything you're going through," she said, and her sincerity was fully apparent. "Not everyone thinks that way...thinks that you're responsible."

"Just the nosy ones," Kate said. "But thanks. I appreciate your standing up for me."

Mary glanced down at the construction paper Kate was holding. "Is that for afternoon kindergarten?" she asked. Kate nodded. Mary held out her hand. "I'll do it for you," she offered. "Heather's in Miss Peck's afternoon class, so I would have been doing it anyway."

"Thanks," Kate answered gratefully. "I just don't understand why they have to be so hateful."

Mary shrugged. "For them, it's easier to be cruel. They would have to actually make an effort to learn the truth and show support. Why do that when you only need to open your mouth to spread gossip? I wouldn't bother with them. Something else will happen and everyone will forget all about you."

Kate chuckled. "Michelle Ryan says the same thing."

"She's right. Just watch. All this will be forgotten soon." Mary took the paper from Kate. "I got this." Kate thanked her and watched her go back toward the volunteer room. Though Kate had never backed down from a fight, she was powerless against the whispers and side-long glances. She'd never been one to indulge in gossip, not because she didn't enjoy a juicy bit of scandal, but because she'd always been taught that to speak ill of someone else meant inviting people to speak ill of you. Her dad was a big one on minding one's own business and growing up she took that to heart.

"Oh, Mary?" she called out. Mary paused at the doorway and looked back. "John's nickname for Diane was Dumb Albino," Kate said.

Mary smirked. "What, not fat?"

Kate gave Mary her own smirk. "Fat was her middle name."

Kate returned to the kindergarten pod in time to pick up Lizzie and take her home.

Lizzie's teacher was gracious about Kate withdrawing her offer to volunteer and Lizzie was surprisingly happy about it. She didn't like having Kate there; it made her feel like less of a big girl, and if there was one thing Lizzie prided herself on, it was that she was now a big girl.

With nothing else to do while the girls were in school, Kate had taken to watching marathons of true crime shows while cleaning her already clean house.

When she finally got her laptop back, she spent her mornings looking up information about John's case and case files for similar crimes. Doug kept her in the loop as much as possible but had little to report. It seemed like the investigation had stalled and Kate despaired that John's murder might never be solved.

Later that afternoon Doug did his best to cheer her up.

"Well, today is a good day," he announced then pushed an envelope across the table.

Kate opened it up then gasped. It was a letter from John's life insurance company stating that they had released the benefit payment and needed wire information to ensure immediate payment.

Kate's eyes teared up. "Oh my God, you don't know what a relief this is."

Doug nodded sympathetically. "I can imagine. And that's not all. The insurance policy John floated through his practice also came through and they want to know where it should go. I'm assuming you don't have a trust set up for the girls yet?"

Through her tears Kate shook her head. "Not for any actual money, no."

"One of the attorneys in my firm handles trusts and estates. I'll ask him to get it set up."

"Thank you," she whispered.

Doug looked at her closely. "Don't you want to know how much it's for?"

Kate looked up. "Oh, I guess so."

"It was a million dollar policy and it also had a double indemnity clause. Each girl will get a million, and since the practice was a corporation and it owned the policy, not John, it's not subject to estate taxes either, so they'll get all of it."

Kate put her face in her hands. She couldn't speak.

"I have to say, John may not have been the best dad or even a decent person but he did right by you guys. I'm impressed," Doug said. Kate nodded through her hands.

"I've got one more thing for you when you're ready," he said.

Kate looked up. "I've won a brand new car?" she joked.

Doug snorted. "No, that part's done with. I talked to my buddy, Tim, the one working on the case? They were trying to identify those three people on the security camera. Two live in the building and one was a guy nobody had ever seen before. At first it looked like he was just moving out, but nobody could identify him."

"I saw them show it on the news. They were asking for him to come forward, right?"

"Yeah," Doug answered. "They're thinking this might be the murderer."

"I haven't heard anything else on the news about this. He could be the murderer. You'd think they'd be eating this up."

Doug snorted. "Not in this county," he said. "They don't want anyone thinking it isn't safe to live here...might lower our property values. Now Baltimore, they'll report every shooting, rape, and break-in like they're proud of it. It's crazy."

Kate hadn't thought of it like that, but Doug had a point. She got up to see him out.

"Thank you so much for everything," she said as she opened the door.

"Thank me after you get my bill," Doug joked. "But seriously. You're not totally out of the woods yet. We'll be able to breathe when they have someone in custody."

Kate agreed. She said goodbye then walked down the street to pick up Lizzie from her bus stop.

TWENTY

With the investigation moving slowly, the lead investigators asked to speak with Kate again, this time at her home where the meeting would be more casual. Kate agreed, and the next morning Doug's friend Tim arrived with the lead investigator, Matt Harmon. They had a woman with them, Carol Sullivan, who Tim introduced as another detective on the case. Doug showed up shortly after their arrival, and Kate settled them in the family room with coffee.

"Thanks for letting us come over like this," Matt began. "I know you've already been interviewed, but since you knew Dr. Richardson the best, I wanted to get a better idea of how all of this looks from your point of view."

Kate didn't know why that mattered, but she was willing to help them in any way she could, so she simply nodded.

"I understand that the last time you saw Dr. Richardson, he was dropping off your daughters after his scheduled weekend with them?"

"Yes," Kate answered.

"And what was his demeanor?"

Kate thought about it for a moment, "He wasn't hostile like he'd been before the custody hearing. I guess he seemed distracted more than anything else."

"Was he normally hostile?"

Kate shook her head. "Not on a regular basis. He had a terrible temper, but he was usually more irritated than outright angry. Small things got on his nerves and he would nitpick or make passive aggressive comments until he either got his way or something else came along to irritate him."

"And what was your relationship like before you divorced?"

"Not great," she admitted. "There was a lot of nitpicking. In fact, I think I got the worst of it because he couldn't be so hypercritical with his patients. They'd leave and go to another dentist if he showed them what he was really like. And his staff all thought he was a good guy, so clearly he saved it until he got home."

"Do you think he may have reverted to his previous behavior patterns with Bethany? The nitpicking and so on?"

Kate shrugged. "Maybe. I never had a conversation with her so I don't really know. All I knew from John was that she'd stopped being the nice girl once they moved in together. I wouldn't be surprised to hear that he'd fallen back into his old habits."

Matt made some notes then looked up. "So nothing else about that day stands out?"

Kate thought about it, shaking her head slowly, but then stopped. "Actually, Bethany wasn't with him."

All three investigators looked at her closely.

"What do you mean, she wasn't with him?" Matt asked.

"Whenever John picked up the girls or dropped them off, Bethany was always with him...except for the last time. She was there when he picked them up but he was alone when he dropped them off."

"And that's unusual?"

Kate nodded so slowly, it wasn't even really a nod but rather an involuntary gesture as she wondered what Bethany's absence meant. "Now that I think about it, it is."

Matt murmured something to Tim who checked his notebook.

"And what time did Dr. Richardson drop the girls off again?"

"Around dinnertime so around six o'clock," she answered, "Why?"

Tim flipped through the pages in his notebook. "Bethany Stephens left for her girlfriend's at five thirty and the video from the condo complex verifies that." The room fell silent as Doug and the investigators ruminated on the details of John's murder.

If Kate were paying attention, she would have felt the room fill with the thick presence of deliberation. Instead, her own thoughts churned through her brain as if trying to regurgitate an errant thought that kept escaping her. When it resurfaced, Kate caught it before it could slip away again. Her brow furrowed. She looked over at Tim and asked, "What time does it say she came back?"

Matt turned and looked at her. "I'm sorry, what was that again?"

Kate rephrased her question. "What time does the video show her coming back?"

Matt and the other investigators looked at each other for a second then Tim got up and quickly left the room. Kate could hear him on his cell phone. She turned and glanced at Doug, who looked back at her with an expression of surprise. A few minutes later Tim returned to the family room shaking his head.

"It's not on there," he said to the room. "They fast forwarded through the entire time after she left. She's not showing up on the video until after the emergency vehicles arrive and it's just her coming out of the building."

Matt and the other detective stood up quickly. "Thank you for your time, Mrs. Richardson," he said politely then the three made a quick exit.

Doug looked impressed. "What made you think of that?" he asked.

Kate shrugged. "I don't know," she answered. "It's been bothering me, yet now it seems like an obvious question. If the video shows her leaving, then it should show when she came back, shouldn't it?"

Doug smiled and shook his head. "Yes, it should. I don't know how much it will matter in the end, but it's certainly an interesting question. At any rate, there are a few things we need to settle, but it won't be with me. Since the insurance company released John's benefit payment, the court released the remainder of his estate to you, so the sale on the practice can proceed and you'll need to decide what you want to do about his condo."

"What do you mean?" Kate asked.

"Well, Bethany hasn't vacated, not once they released the crime scene. She resumed residence there once the investigators and Medical Examiner's office was done with it," Doug answered.

"You mean she's still living there?"

Doug nodded. "Yes, but she doesn't own it. It goes to you as the beneficiary of his estate."

Kate felt conflicted. As much as she resented Bethany for putting herself where she didn't belong, John was to blame for the breakup of their marriage. She didn't want to be responsible for Bethany being homeless either.

"Where is Bethany from?" Kate asked.

Doug looked through his notebook. "Curtis Bay. Her mother still lives there."

Kate knew Curtis Bay was a neighborhood in Baltimore only twenty minutes away.

"Then sell it," she said. "Bethany can go live with her mother."

Doug nodded then left to follow up with his buddy Tim so Kate set off down the street to pick up Lizzie from the bus stop. She arrived just as the bus pulled up and was glad to be spared any more conversation about John's murder. The women on the street were nice to her face, for the most part, but Kate knew many conversations had taken place behind her back.

Lizzie hopped off and skipped alongside her on the way home.

Annabelle came over to babysit so Kate could facilitate the first meeting of her new group. When she opened the door though, the girl looked positively forlorn.

"Is everything OK?" she asked as she let Annabelle in.

Annabelle shrugged. "Just mom problems."

Kate was sympathetic. Annabelle's mother, Pam, was a difficult woman who made no secret that her son Brian was her sun and moon. She couldn't begin to imagine how that made Annabelle feel.

"I'm sorry about that," she said sincerely. "Well the girls are thrilled you're here." Sure enough, both girls came running as soon as Kate called them down.

"We have a WiiU!" Lizzie announced and grabbed Annabelle's hand to pull her toward the basement stairs.

"I ordered a pizza. The money is on the counter," she called after them. Annabelle waved and let the girls pull her off.

Kate called out her goodbyes then left for her support meeting.

Kate was surprised to see a number of cars at the church when she pulled up. She wondered if one of the earlier meetings had run long. Inside, she saw a considerable number of women already seated in the meeting room. The only face she recognized was Evelyn's. Curious, she checked the door and indeed a sign reading 'Widowed After Divorce' hung on the meeting room door. She bypassed the meeting room and stepped into the office where she found a large stack of papers with a post-it on top with her name written on it. She dropped off her bag and grabbed the stack. Voices fell away when she stepped into the room, and Kate suddenly felt extremely self-conscious as she made her way to the only available chair in the circle.

"Good evening everyone," she said as she sat down. "My name is Kate Richardson and I will be your facilitator for this evening." She was relieved that the women were at least smiling at her, even Evelyn who normally functioned in a mental fog.

"Is everyone here for 'Widowed After Divorce'?" she asked and received nods all around as an answer. "OK, wow. Well, since this is our first meeting, why don't we go around and say our names and what brought us here? I'll go first." She took a deep breath before launching into an abbreviated version of her history. "As I said before, my name is Kate. I was married for eleven years when my husband left me to pursue a relationship with another woman. He passed away just recently and I am currently dealing with the fallout from his death." Kate looked around and saw sympathetic nods from all the women. "Why don't we go around the circle? Would you like to introduce yourself?" she said to the woman closest to her.

The woman looked startled, obviously not expecting to be called on.

"Oh, I didn't realize we were going to be sharing our information," she said. "I thought this was more like a lecture."

"Well, technically we're a support group," Kate said politely. "Our goal is to discuss what emotional and practical issues we might be experiencing and how to best address and overcome the obstacles in front of us."

"Oh, of course...well, my name is Jessica Bailey and um...Well, I'm not really divorced so..." she began then trailed off into silence.

Kate was confused. "But you're widowed?"

The other woman turned red with mortification. "Not exactly," she replied.

Kate looked around at the other women and noted that most of them looked uncomfortable too. "Is anyone widowed?" she asked and everyone but Evelyn shook their heads. "Divorced?" she ventured and got the same result. Poor Evelyn looked like Kate felt.

"I don't understand," she said to the room. "If you're not divorced or widowed then why are you here?" She looked at Jessica first who immediately looked to the other women for help but her silent plea went unanswered as the other women looked away in embarrassment. She was an even more alarming shade of red when she turned back to face Kate.

"We...um...just wanted to meet...you?" she ventured.

Kate was stunned. "Did you think I was going to talk about my ex-husband's murder?"

The nods around the circle were slow in coming, but eventually everyone but Evelyn admitted the truth.

Kate felt a sudden burst of pain in her temples that she desperately wanted to rub. She fought to keep the irritation out of her voice and asked, "Even if that's a subject I was willing to share, why would you think that's relevant to a support group?" No one had an answer.

Jessica, the unofficial spokesperson for the group, spoke up. "I guess that's why we thought it would be a lecture format instead of...well....a support group format."

"So all of you are here because you were curious about my ex-husband's murder?"

Again, nods all around.

"Is anyone here for support?"

Evelyn was the only person to raise her hand.

"Thank you, Evelyn," Kate said with a weak smile. "Listen, I don't know what gave you the impression that I would share the details of my current situation, and to be honest I'm not sure what I can say right now anyway. But just to satisfy your curiosity, I did not murder my husband, the police are doing a thorough investigation and it is my understanding that they will be making an arrest soon. And it's not me. If you have any kind of issues you need to work out, you are welcome to stay. The rest may go."

Kate sat back and waited as the majority of extremely embarrassed women got up and left the meeting room, including Jessica.

Only a handful remained and Kate looked at them pointedly.

"You did say any kind of issues, right?"

Kate nodded. "Yes," she answered tiredly, "any kind of issue. Would you like to start?"

By the end of the session, Kate was glad to have invited the others to stay. Of the women that were left, two were suffering some serious emotional abuse, one was struggling emotionally from a previous rape assault, and the other had an alarming shopping addiction. Since their issues were so varied, Kate promised to look into finding support groups that might be more suitable for them. Evelyn remained in her chair as the other women left.

"Evelyn, are you OK?" she asked.

"Oh, I'm all right. I just wanted to make sure you were all right."

Kate sat down next to Evelyn and sighed. "I'll be OK when all of this is over."

Evelyn nodded then reached over and took Kate's hand.

"When Harris died, I felt like I lost my best friend," Evelyn said quietly then chuckled. "He was a terrible friend, but I'm still going to miss him."

Kate smiled and wondered if she should be missing John. He'd been so awful toward the end that the divorce was more a relief than a heart break. It wasn't until his death that she realized how used to him she'd become.

"I read the story they wrote in the newspaper," Evelyn continued. "It doesn't seem like they know who did it."

Kate gave Evelyn a grim smile. "They investigated me first."

Evelyn nodded. "Of course they would. Men always think we're the 'woman scorned' and all we want to do is get back at them, don't they? They don't realize how much quieter it is when they aren't around."

Kate smiled. "You're right. They do think they know everything. But I was just thinking that I should be more upset that John is dead but...I really just feel...numb, I guess."

Evelyn considered this. "Bad marriages are like a bad tooth. It's a constant pain that always hurts, but over time you don't notice the pain as much. But when the tooth is pulled and the pain is completely gone, you wonder how you put up with it for so long. His being dead doesn't change that."

Kate smiled. "That's exactly how it feels." She took a closer look at Evelyn. "Are you feeling all right?"

"Oh, I'm fine. It's the medication they gave me. Anti-depressants and other things."

"You're not driving home, are you?"

"Oh Lord no. My daughter is coming to pick me up," Evelyn laughed then stood. "She's probably waiting for me outside." Evelyn picked up her handbag and hung it on her arm. "Are you going to be all right?"

Kate smiled at the irony and walked Evelyn outside. "I'll be fine. Thank you for listening."

Evelyn's daughter was already waiting in the car. Evelyn turned and patted Kate's hand. "That's the whole point of the support group, isn't it?" she asked. "To offer support?"

Kate watched Evelyn's daughter help her mother into the car and waved as they drove off.

Since it was the weekend, Patrick came by to spend some time with her and the girls. Her heart, and other parts of her, gave a little lurch at the sight of him standing on the front steps, but things still felt weird. Lizzie and Emma were happy to see him and excited to show off their newfound talents on the game system Kate had bought them.

Patrick gave her a quick kiss and followed the girls downstairs.

Kate made herself a cup of coffee and sat in the breakfast room. She could hear Patrick and the girls playing in the basement. It made her smile. With some time to herself, Kate called the church for some direction on where to send the women who legitimately needed help. Instead of information, the reception volunteer asked if Kate was available to come in sometime next week to meet with the clergy about the future of "Widowed After Divorce." Kate was mortified that she was going to be fired from her volunteer position but agreed to be there on Monday.

She put on a brave face when Patrick brought the girls upstairs for something to eat.

"How about we go out for an early dinner and go see a movie?" he offered. The girls enthusiastically agreed.

Kate smiled. "That sounds good. Where should we go?"

"Taco Bell!" Lizzie suggested at full volume.

Kate and Patrick laughed. "How about something a little less Taco Bellish? Like Oishii Sushi?" Patrick asked

"I love sushi!" Lizzie announced. She ran to get her shoes on. Emma put on a patient expression and followed her sister to help.

"Are you sure you want to go out?" Patrick asked. "You don't look very excited about it."

"I'm sorry. Things aren't going well right now and I can't seem to let it go. People keep looking at me like I'm going to pull out a knife and start decapitating people."

Patrick moved closer to her and wrapped his arms around her. "I'm sorry. I thought it might be nice for you to get out and do something fun."

"I appreciate that." Kate tried to smile.

In the end, it was fun. The sushi restaurant was very good and the wait staff couldn't have been kinder and more patient with the girls. They were all very impressed that such young non-Asian children loved sushi. The sushi chef even came out with crisp white chef hats for the girls to wear. After dinner, they went to see Disney's latest installment at the theater. Though Kate didn't necessarily enjoy the movie, it felt good to be holding Patrick's hand in the dark. They had spent so little time together recently that when they were finally together, Kate realized how much she missed him.

By the time they got home, both Kate and the girls were exhausted. Patrick waited downstairs while Kate put the girls to bed.

He was sitting in the family room when she came back down.

"I can't stay much longer," he said as he jumped up. "My mom is having a birthday party for my dad, and I'm expected to be there."

Kate's smile was tired. "Of course you should be there."

"I wish I could ask you to come along. I'd really like for you to meet everyone," he said.

"I appreciate that, but I'm not sure that's a good idea...with everything that's going on."

Patrick nodded. "Yeah, we should probably wait. I'll call you tomorrow?"

This time Kate nodded. She gave him a quick kiss and saw him to the door. As she watched Patrick drive away, she wondered what had changed in their relationship and if the change was in him...or in her.

On Monday, Kate pulled into the parking lot near the church offices and went in. One of the reception volunteers, a wonderfully kind and wickedly funny woman named Barbara, looked up and smiled.

"Oh, good morning, Kate! Are you here for an appointment?" she asked.

"Yes. I think I'm supposed to meet with Reverend Jess?"

"Go on back then. I think the clergy are all in the library." Barbara waved toward the door at the end of the hallway.

Reverend Jess was in the church library with the two other clergy that served the parish. Reverend Joyce was the head rector and Father Stephen was another associate rector whose focus was on adult ministries within the church. All three looked up when Kate appeared in the doorway.

"Oh, Kate!" Reverend Jess jumped up. "Come in! We were just talking about you."

Kate took the seat Jess had indicated. Reverend Joyce gave her a kind smile.

"Don't look so worried," she said gently. "Would you like something to drink?"

Kate shook her head. "I feel like I've been called to the principal's office," she joked.

The clergy chuckled appreciatively. "It's nothing like that," Reverend Joyce reassured her. "We did want to talk to you about the other night though."

Kate's heart sank. "You heard?" she asked. They all nodded.

"Evelyn Carroll came to see us. She was concerned that you might have been...how shall I say it...taken aback by the rampant curiosity of some of our parishioners."

"It was surprising," Kate admitted. "But I can't really blame them. We live in a climate of too much information. It's only natural they'd want to satisfy their curiosity when the source is so available. Besides, some of the women who came actually need help so it wasn't a total loss."

"That's very generous of you, Kate," Joyce replied, "which leads me to the reason we asked you here today. Evelyn has suggested, and we think it's a great idea, that you might be better served working with parishioners one-on-one rather than in a group setting." Reverend Joyce put her hand up before Kate could interrupt. "Now don't get me wrong, the work you did with your previous group was wonderful, and the surveys that came back from the participants all had great things to say about you. But for the time being, and maybe permanently, we'd like to offer you the opportunity to provide counseling services here at the church."

"You mean see patients here at the church?" Kate asked. It was not what she was expecting.

Reverend Joyce nodded. "The church had originally provided a space for pastoral counseling services many years ago and we are in a position to resume the program. Given the climate in today's world, it's long overdue. You'll work with our own parishioners as well as patients recommended through the diocese. You can bill privately until you are credentialed with the insurance companies and we have space available in Rose Hill so you'll have some privacy."

"I'm sorry to sound stupid but do you mean to suggest that I set up my own practice? Here?" Kate couldn't believe her ears. Private counseling had always been her dream, and now it was being offered like a gift from God.

Reverend Joyce tilted her head at her. "Yes...why? Is there a problem?"

"No...it's just...this isn't what I was expecting. This is a huge surprise." Kate admitted.

"Good surprise or bad surprise?" Reverend Jess joked.

Kate laughed. "Great surprise, but are you sure you want me here? I mean, won't my having gone through a still unresolved murder investigation...raise some eyebrows?"

Reverend Joyce leaned over and placed her hand over Kate's in a gesture of comfort.

"We've met with the Vestry to discuss this exact issue and it's been determined that since you've been exonerated by the sheriff's department, there's no reason not to continue with our original plan. Unless there's something you need to tell us?"

Kate shook her head. "No, nothing."

"That's wonderful then," Reverend Joyce answered. "Jess here can show you your new space and get you set up."

"Thank you so much," Kate said, her gratitude heartfelt. "I can't tell you how much I appreciate this." She stood and shook hands with the other woman, though she really wanted to hug her. Reverend Joyce couldn't know how much Kate needed this.

"I think we should be thanking you. We've been looking for a way to fully serve our members in crisis and with you on board, we'll be able to do that. We'll meet again next week to see how things are going, all right?"

Kate nodded and followed Reverend Jess out the door.

"Since the old rectory has been converted to offices for the school, Joyce thought the second floor of Rose Hill would work well for you," Reverend Jess said as they walked across the church's campus.

Rose Hill was a large farmhouse situated on the far end of the campus. A garden and mature trees surrounded it.

"I thought someone lived there," Kate remarked.

"Not for a while now. The third floor is still an apartment but the second floor has been broken up into offices. You'll still have a full kitchen in your space."

They reached the side door of Rose Hill. Reverend Jess unlocked it and handed Kate the set of keys.

"You have the key to this door and a key for your office there. Some of the staff used to have offices here so there's already a copy and fax machine in here for you to use."

Kate followed her up the interior stairs and into the main door to the second level.

Though the house didn't seem big on the outside, there was a surprising amount of space. Just to their left was a small but serviceable kitchen and to the right a sitting area that was probably the living room when it was still an apartment. Since the original interior stairs ran up the side of the house rather than the center, the remaining area was divided into rooms with a full bath in the corner. To be honest, it looked just like a country doctor's office with ancient wooden floors and plain walls.

"I'm sorry the furniture isn't much. We use what we inherit."

Kate smiled. "It's lovely. I think it'll work just fine."

Reverend Jess pulled her own keys out of her pocket and opened all of the interior doors.

"You have your pick of offices. I know Joyce intends to bring in more counselors but I'm not sure when that's going to happen, so you'll be on your own for at least a little bit."

Kate and Reverend Jess stood in the small space and looked around.

"So...what do you think?" Reverend Jess asked.

"Thank you," she said sincerely. "With all that's been going on, I didn't expect this. To be honest, I thought you were going to relieve me of my support group duties."

Reverend Jess looked sympathetic. "This must be really hard on you."

Kate sighed. "The worst part is the waiting. It feels like nothing is happening...or progressing. It's like John's murder has pushed everything into some sort of weird limbo. I realize the police have to take their time with the investigation, but it keeps everything else at a standstill while the rest of the world speculates on what really happened and passes judgment."

"It is. And that's why I'm so thankful for this opportunity," Kate said. "It gives me the chance to step away from my own problems and help someone else. I can't thank you enough."

Reverend Jess chuckled. "You should probably thank Evelyn Carroll. It was originally her idea, and since she's a considerable benefactor of this church, they're going to take her suggestions very seriously."

Kate was surprised. Evelyn was a kind woman, but she always seemed so out of it. Who knew she wielded so much power?

Reverend Jess made a move to leave. "I've got bible study in a few minutes, so let me know if there is anything else you might need. Father Stephen will be your clergy representative, but as far as the lay staff is concerned, you're the acting head of Pastoral Care and Counseling until the program is formalized. They'll make your position more formal. You might be invited to speak to the vestry every so often, but that won't happen for a while. We have a young woman, Hillary, who has taken some time off from seminary and has offered to function as a part-time receptionist, so we'll get a desk set up for her. Carl will be coming by to put up your signage sometime tomorrow. All your phones are up and running, but we don't have computers in here yet since your system will need to be completely separate from the church's network."

"That's fine. I can take care of getting a computer since I'll need to set up an electronic health record system," Kate said. "And thanks for the title. It makes me feel important."

Reverend Jess chuckled. "You are important. Besides, it's the least we could do." She moved over to the door and opened it. "If you need me, I'll be in the Parish Life Center."

Kate thanked her then turned to survey her new digs.

Of the rooms available, Kate decided on one that had been painted a soft gray. It was the smallest of the three but had a large window that overlooked the garden of the house next door to the church property. Its desk had been moved closer to the window and hugged the wall leaving her plenty of room to seat people comfortably. She checked the bathroom and kitchen and noted that each needed supplies, so she scrounged a piece of scrap paper from one of the other desks and made a list. When she was done, she locked the door behind her and walked to her car.

By the time she'd finished her shopping, it was time to pick up Lizzie from the bus stop. Kate pulled into her driveway then walked the short distance to the bus stop just as the bus was pulling up.

Kate smiled listening to Lizzie recount the excitement that was Kindergarten but stopped her short at the sight of an unfamiliar car parked in front of their house. As she slowly walked towards her drive-way, she was dismayed to see Bethany's mother climbing out of the car. Kate cut through the front yard and quickly opened the front door.

"Why don't you go see what's on TV?" She nudged Lizzie into the house. She let the storm door slam behind her and watched as the other woman slowly made her way up Kate's walkway. Kate gripped her cell phone inside her pocket and thumbed redial, hoping Doug would answer right way.

"What are you doing here?" Kate asked loudly as soon as she heard Doug's voice answer. "I don't need any more trouble from you or your daughter." Her phone went quiet, and she was relieved that he understood the need for subterfuge. Kate pulled her phone out so he could hear the other woman better.

"Now, there's no need for that," the other woman answered, her tone conciliatory, her hands out as if showing she had come unarmed. "I think we just got off on the wrong foot. I'm Shauna, by the way." Shauna held out her hand as if to offer it to Kate, but she was standing far enough away that Kate would have to come down her steps to accept, and that certainly wasn't going to happen. Instead, Kate ignored Shauna's hand and stared at her. Out of the corner of her eye, she could see Doug quickly coming up the street with his cell phone to his ear. When he spotted Shauna, he took a hard right into the neighbor's yard. Kate assumed that he was coming up the side of the house through the backyard in order to eavesdrop unseen.

"I guess you're not gonna shake my hand, huh," Shauna stated flatly. Kate just stared at her. Shauna looked like an older, heavier version of Bethany. She had the same brown hair and large brown eyes, but where Bethany's hair was long and straight, Shauna's had been permed too many times. Limp ringlets hung around her face while her roots were arrow straight. And where Bethany was quite pretty, Shauna's weight distorted her beauty making her look swollen and pig-like. From the web of broken capillaries across her nose, Kate suspected alcohol was Shauna's best friend.

"I understand that you might not be real happy to see me but I think it's only fair that you listen to what I gotta say," Shauna said. Kate remained silent, and Shauna took that as a sign to continue. "First, you gotta appreciate that I need to defend my girl from those names you called her. Isn't nice to call someone a whore...especially when she's just lost her man and all."

Kate bristled. "That was my mother-in-law and she is entitled to her opinion," she said through clenched teeth.

"Well, her opinion is wrong," Shauna snapped.

"Opinions are never wrong. That's why they're opinions and not facts," Kate countered. "Why are you here exactly?"

"I think you know why I'm here." Shauna attempted to sound more reasonable, but it came out sly and insinuating. "Listen, I know what it's like when a man thinks he can set you aside. But the fact is your man made his choice when he divorced you. Now you're takin' everything away from my girl when it's all rightfully hers and I think you know that."

"Your daughter seduced a married man," Kate said, trying to keep her voice steady. "She made his choice very easy for him. But I'm not sure what you think I'm taking away from her or what she is entitled to...they weren't married, and as far as I know they weren't even engaged. When your daughter tried to get him to change his will and life insurance, he kept *me* as beneficiary...even after they were together. I think that clearly speaks to his intentions regarding his relationship with your daughter."

Shauna's eyes narrowed. "You don't need to take that tone with me," she said. "I'm not stupid. They had an agreement, and they *was* going to get married. That means she still gets...what's it called...*palimony.*" Shauna ended her statement looking triumphant at having pulled palimony out of her tiny little brain. "So you gotta just face the facts and do the right thing." She waved her hand toward Kate's house. "All this rightfully belongs to Bethany. She says she's already told you a million times."

Kate kept her voice level. "There is no palimony law in Maryland. A quick Google search could have told you that. But that's beside the point. I'm quite aware what Bethany thinks. She's made that *loud* and clear..."

Shauna interrupted her with a chuckle. "That girl has a temper on her, I'll give you that. Just like her sister, Victoria. But it ain't ever got her in trouble like it has her sister 'cause Bethany's smart. She knows when she's right. Look, I'm tryin' to be reasonable here..."

"What's reasonable about showing up at my home to tell me I don't have a right to be here? How is it that you and your idiot daughter think that she's entitled to anything? Was this her plan all along? Kill John and get all his stuff when they weren't even married? She can't be that smart if she doesn't even understand basic inheritance laws."

Kate watched Shauna's face turn beet red. "My girl ain't never killed nobody! She's heartbroken to lose her man like that. And now you wanna throw her out of her own house? He bought that condo for her!" Shauna was in full rant by then.

Kate stared at the woman screaming at her and realized Shauna could potentially be dangerous. At that moment Doug stepped around the corner and made his way through the yard to Kate's side.

"Who the fuck is this?" Shauna screamed, spittle flying from her mouth.

"This is my attorney," Kate answered.

Shauna's mouth clamped shut, and her face turned purple. "I'm not done with you," she growled.

"Oh, I think you are," Kate answered then watched with great satisfaction as Shauna stomped off and got into her car. She and Doug stared as Shauna gunned her engine and peeled off down the road.

Doug let out a breath. "God, what a family. Are you OK?"

Kate nodded. "Surprisingly, I feel fine. But I need to check on Lizzie. What if she heard all that?"

"Lizzie's fine," Doug reassured her. "Christine went in through the back door with the kids and they're playing in the basement."

Kate let out a sigh of relief. "Thank God. And I really need to thank you. This was above and beyond the call of duty."

Doug laughed. "Even if you weren't paying me, I wouldn't have missed that for the world. It's like the worst reality TV, except it's in your front yard."

Kate almost laughed then sobered at the truth of his statement. Her life *had* turned into the worst kind of television and she felt her face turn red with embarrassment.

They found Lizzie showing the two youngest McAvoy children the WiiU while Christine stood by watching them. She looked over as they came down the steps, her expression worried.

"Everything OK now?" she asked. Doug nodded.

"Everything's fine."

Kate went over to Christine and hugged her. "Thank you so much for looking after Lizzie. I really didn't want that woman in the house."

Christine laughed. "God no," she said. She pulled away and smiled at Kate. "And it was no problem at all. The real problem is how to get these kids home now."

The adults chuckled as the McAvoys gathered their children, bid their goodbyes, and left.

By the time Emma came home from school, Kate was experiencing a delayed reaction from Shauna's visit. With no one to rant to, she struggled to calm her nerves so as not to upset her girls. She found herself reaching for the wine then chided herself for using alcohol as a crutch. Instead, she settled the girls in their rooms and sank into one of the overstuffed chairs in the family room to close her eyes. It wasn't long before the stress of the last few weeks took its toll on her energy and she was asleep.

TWENTY ONE

The next day, Kate dropped off the girls at school then drove to the church to set up her new office then used her new phone to follow up with the handful of women she'd met at her last support group effort. She was surprised and pleased that all of them wanted to make appointments, one as early as the next morning. She set out stacks of new patient forms on the small table near the entrance.

When she was done Kate sat quietly in her new office and looked around. She'd pulled two of the armchairs in from the living room for her patients and was pleasantly surprised that the faded upholstery worked nicely against the gray walls. She moved them so they were together but not crowded and pulled a small side table from one of the other offices and placed it between them. A little more art on the walls and the space would be perfect.

The house was large enough that from her office she could hear very little road noise coming from the main road. She knew she would get some noise from the playground situated directly behind the house, but she figured the sounds of children playing might actually serve as a soothing backdrop to her therapy efforts.

With a last look around, Kate smiled at the new direction her life had taken, then left.

Since it was so close to the time the bus came, Kate stopped her SUV at the bus stop and waited. She felt her phone ping and pulled it out of her pocket. It was a text message from Patrick. She smiled. It was more affectionate than suggestive, telling her how much he missed her. The departure from sexting was a change that made Kate feel good about their relationship. She was still smiling when Lizzie got off the bus.

The next morning was her first official day as a pastoral care counselor. Kate reported for work and found her first patient, Holly, already there waiting. Hillary gave her an apologetic look.

Kate waved the young woman over. She smiled shyly as Kate unlocked her office door.

"I hope you don't mind, but I got here earlier so Hillary let me in," Holly said. "I filled out the forms while I was waiting."

Kate smiled and accepted her paperwork. "It's fine. I'm sorry if I kept you waiting long. Would you like some coffee or tea?"

Holly shook her head and stood. "No thanks. If I have any more caffeine, I won't be able to function the rest of the day."

Kate smiled politely then waved Holly toward the armchair.

"I know we didn't have much of a chance to talk during our group time," Kate began. "How about we start with a little bit of your history?"

Holly's smile turned strained and Kate could tell she felt uncomfortable.

"It's OK," Kate reassured her. "This is a completely judgment-free room. I only want to help you."

She watched as Holly's shoulders relaxed as the tension drained away.

Holly took a deep breath then began.

"I guess I've always been a shopper," she said. "But now it's turned into a real problem." Holly paused, her expression a mix of shame and embarrassment.

Kate was sympathetic. She gave Holly a smile of encouragement.

"Tell me how you feel when you go shopping," Kate offered.

An hour later, Holly looked exhausted but Kate felt good about her chances. She had come clean about her addiction to shopping and though Kate knew it was extremely difficult to break the cycle of addiction to something everyone does on a daily basis, Holly seemed committed to recovery. Kate suggested Holly attend a twelve-step program along with private counseling and they made a plan to meet regularly. She also gave Holly some coping strategies and advised her to call if she felt the overwhelming urge to spend. They agreed to meet the following Monday and Kate promised to have additional support materials available then. Holly thanked her then impulsively reached over and gave Kate a hug.

"Thank you so much," Holly said breathlessly. "I feel like you're saving my life."

Kate stiffened for a moment then relaxed and returned her hug. "You deserve credit for your own recovery," she assured the other woman. "You've already crossed the biggest hurdle by coming here."

Holly pulled away and wiped at her eyes. "Still, this is huge for me. My husband was ready to bail on me if I didn't come today."

Kate led her to the door. "But you did come and that took a lot of courage and determination to make a positive change. I think you're going to do great."

Holly thanked Kate again then left.

Since she didn't have any other patients scheduled for the day, Kate sent Hillary home and left soon after.

On Saturday, Kate let the girls sleep in while she cleaned the house. She was just finishing the kitchen when her cell phone went off. It was a text from Michelle.

Turn on the news.

Kate stepped into the family room and turned on the TV. The weather was on. She wondered why Michelle wanted her to watch the weather when there was a knock on the door. Kate turned to see Michelle letting herself in.

"You really need to keep your door locked," she said in a rush then hurried to Kate's side. "Did you see it? Has it come back on yet?"

"See what? The weather?" Kate answered.

Michelle was out of breath. She must have run all the way up the street. "They just announced the story. It should be on next."

The two women stood and waited through several commercials and a human interest segment then another commercial, Michelle growing more and more impatient.

"Come on, come on, come on," she whispered. "Oh my God! Who cares about bladder protection pads...wait, here it is!"

Kate and Michelle both stared at the morning news anchor who'd come on the screen.

"Shocking news coming out of Howard County this morning...Howard County Police have made an arrest in the murder of Dr. John Richardson. Dr. Richardson was found stabbed to death this past August by his girlfriend, Bethany Stephens. Police have arrested Ms. Stephens for the murder, citing Dr. Richardson's insurance money as a motive. She's expected to be indicted later this week. Bob Brown is reporting live from the Howard County courthouse. Bob?"

Kate held her breath as the on-site reporter popped up on the screen. He was standing in front of the courthouse.

"Thanks Carol. Breaking news from here in Howard County; the investigation into the murder of a prominent local dentist, Dr. John Richardson, appears to have ended."

The screen cut away to a prerecorded video of Matt Harmon leading a cuffed Bethany to a waiting patrol car. It was still dark in the video and Bethany looked like she was wearing pajamas.

Kate and Michelle both stared at the television, their eyes wide.

"Howard County investigators made a visit early this morning to serve a warrant for the arrest of Bethany Stephens. She has been charged with first-degree murder in the stabbing death of Dr. John Richardson, a local dentist and community leader in Ellicott City, Maryland. Ms. Stephens was taken into custody early this morning and the state's attorney expects an indictment will be handed down soon."

The screen cut back to Bob Brown for the live report.

"Investigators allege that money *is* likely one of the motives in Dr. Richardson's murder. We'll keep you up to date as this story unfolds. Carol?"

Kate turned off the television just as her phone rang. It was Doug.

"I just saw it," she said.

"I'll be right over."

"This is best day ever," Kate said.

"The *best* day ever?" Michelle asked.

Kate laughed. "Well, maybe not the *best* day but certainly in the top five...or maybe ten."

Michelle smiled as Doug let himself in.

"You really should keep that locked," he said as he made his way into the family room.

"So I've been told."

"So, Tim called me last night letting me know that they were going to bring Bethany in. He's concerned that her mother's going to show up here attempting some form of retaliation so they're putting a guy out front to make sure nothing happens."

"Really?" Kate asked. "I didn't see a patrol car outside when I took out the trash."

Doug shook his head. "It's an unmarked car and they're down in front of the Shay's house. I think they're hoping she shows up here so they can bring her in too. They're wondering if she knew a lot more about John's death than she should."

Kate nodded.

"Anyway," Doug continued, "Tim told me they found the unidentified guy on the tape. Apparently he's some kind of boyfriend or ex of Bethany's who was there to pick up some of his stuff. When they served the search warrant for the boyfriend's apartment, they found the boxes he'd supposedly picked up from her. In it was the knife she used with her prints all over it and a gray hoodie that showed trace blood evidence on it. DNA confirmed it was John's blood, and when they checked the tape, they saw an individual in a gray hoodie returning not long after Bethany supposedly left. They originally thought it was the kid next door but they're pretty sure the person on the tape is actually Bethany."

"But they can't be sure," Kate said.

Doug shrugged. "Not for sure, no. But now that they have the possible murder weapon and the sweatshirt, it's just another factor in their case to prove premeditation. And they've already determined that her alibi was totally false. Bethany lying about her whereabouts proves consciousness of guilt. Their case against her is as tight as it's going to get. There's no way she's going weasel out of this."

Kate started to worry. "But there's still a chance, right? She could try to pin it on that guy or something."

Doug smirked. "I guarantee she's going to try to pin it on him, and for all we know he *is* guilty, or at least some sort of accomplice. But she's not without some culpability in this. The case is definitely circumstantial, but it's a very strong case nonetheless."

Doug leaned over and not quite reaching Kate, put his hand on the armrest next to her. "Listen. It's not our job to run the investigation. The detectives assigned to John's case are very good and they are doing their jobs very well. Our main goal here was to protect you, to keep *you* out of those handcuffs. And we did."

Kate nodded, and Michelle looked at her sympathetically.

Doug chuckled. "The timing to all of this couldn't be better. The sheriff's office was supposed to enforce the eviction order today. Now you can get rid of everything and sell the place."

Michelle chuckled appreciatively while Kate simply asked, "Is there someone we can hire to do that? There's nothing there that I would want to keep and I'd rather not go in."

Doug nodded. "I'll call a removal company and get all that taken care of. We can donate all of the household items and store the rest. That sound good?"

Kate nodded.

Doug looked at his watch. "I've got to get back to the house. Christine needs to leave for her mother's. Call me if anything comes up, OK?"

Kate thanked him and saw him out. When she returned to the family room, Michelle had turned the television back on and was watching a repeat of the earlier newscast.

"Somehow this feels like it isn't over," Kate said as she sat down next to Michelle.

"That's just the pessimism talking," Michelle answered. "It's like Doug said, they have so much evidence against her, there's no way she could get off."

"Still," Kate murmured. "I just get this feeling like it's never going to end."

And it didn't. Once news of Bethany's arrest made its way through the neighborhood, residents were surprisingly divided. There were those who had sided with Kate all along and were vocal in their support and there were those who actually sided with Bethany and accused Kate of not only murdering her husband but framing an innocent girl. And despite the fact that the group who considered Kate guilty was considerably smaller, their message was loud and clear.

Even Michelle was surprised by it. When she stopped by one morning after volunteering at the school, Kate was surprised at how angry she was.

"You will never guess what I just heard," Michelle said as she stomped into the house.

"I'm a murderer," Kate answered dully then closed the door behind her.

"Oh my God!" Michelle cried. "How can these women be so stupid?"

Kate sighed. "So what happened?"

Michelle took a breath and looked at her friend. "Never mind...forget I said anything. It's just little minds with big mouths."

"Let me guess, Diane and her friends," Kate said.

Michelle's expression turned gloomy. "Yeah."

"I'm not surprised." She led Michelle to the kitchen and offered her a seat at the counter. "They had me convicted the minute they heard

John was dead. He could have died from a heart attack and they still would have said it was my fault."

"I'm sorry," Michelle said quietly.

"I just don't understand it," Kate's voice went up in frustration. "Do people here really hate me that much?"

Michelle shook her head. "No, no one hates you, Kate. They just lead shitty little lives and take too much enjoyment when someone else's life turns to shit. People like Diane and the women who suck up to her...well, I want to call them insecure but that makes them sound like we should be sympathetic. What I really want to say is that they're stupid and small-minded. They haven't accomplished anything of any real significance and they know it. But instead of elevating themselves, they drag others down. They function on the level of middle school mean girls. I shouldn't be so surprised; she's done this before, you know."

Kate's eyebrows went up. "Done what, gossip? That's hardly a shocker."

Michelle snorted. "No...well yes, she's always done that, but I mean the mean girl thing. She periodically picks out some poor unsuspecting mom and makes her life miserable. She did it to a woman who moved just down the street from her a few years ago. She started out nice and friendly and when the woman confided little things that annoyed her...like her next door neighbor's dog barking too much, Diane lied and exaggerated her comment and turned what was really just a petty annoyance into World War Three. Diane had the whole street shunning this poor woman."

Kate was shocked. That was an atrocious thing to do. She'd never realized Diane was that horrible of a person.

"What happened to the woman?" she asked.

"They left." Michelle answered simply. "It got to the point where it was hurting their kids so they listed their house and moved. There was another neighbor a few years ago that lived in Diane's old neighborhood who said she did the same thing there. It's like Diane can't be happy unless she's making someone else miserable."

Kate's clinical mind kicked in. "Diane sounds like a sociopath," she said more to herself than to Michelle.

"Seriously? Isn't that dangerous?" Michelle looked truly frightened.

Kate took a deep breath. "Not physically dangerous but definitely psychologically and socially dangerous. And it's not like she can be cured of it. The only way to deal with a sociopath is to avoid them. Or beat them at their own game."

"How would you beat them at their own game?" Michelle's expression turned skeptical. "They're insane right?"

"They can be either sane or insane. Insane just means they lack a certain level of understanding that what they are doing is wrong, that they aren't necessarily responsible for their actions. But sociopaths are very high functioning. They know exactly what they are doing; they just don't care how it affects others."

Michelle looked concerned. "Then how do you deal with them?"

"Sociopaths need their egos fed constantly. They manipulate people into thinking they are smart or socially powerful and they thrive on fear. You start chipping away at the number of people who believe them by pointing out the lies that they tell, eventually they lose all of their social support and the people who are afraid of getting on their bad side will see there's nothing to be afraid of. With nothing to feed their egos, they have to change tactics or leave."

"I say we take her down then," Michelle raged. "What she's doing is complete bullshit."

Kate shrugged. "All I can do is not give her any more ammunition. She's already lied and misrepresented things. The only response is to challenge her credibility. If I get upset and confront her, it'll look to her like she's won. If I stay away from her or just ignore her like she doesn't matter, it'll drive her insane and she'll over-respond. Normal people will realize how unhinged she is and start to avoid her. Eventually, she'll turn on her closest friends and they'll avoid her too. Once everyone has turned away from her, she loses."

Michelle looked doubtful. "Then what? Does she learn her lesson?"

Kate looked sad. "No. She'll never stop behaving this way. She'll lick her wounds then move on to another victim. Sociopaths are power hungry; they prey on the weak. If they feel like you have more power than they do, they'll avoid you and move on to someone they perceive as powerless."

Michelle looked thoughtful. "I wonder if that's what she did to Sandra and Todd."

"Her neighbors?" Kate asked. "I heard she split them up."

"She did," Michelle answered. "But she and Sandra were really good friends for years. They did everything together and went everywhere together. Then one day, boom, Diane tells her that she and Todd are going to get married and Sandra has to move out."

Kate snorted. "That sounds familiar."

"I know, right?" Michelle exclaimed. "Anyway, Sandra saw the writing on the wall and forced Todd to sell the house in the divorce so Diane couldn't just move in. Unfortunately Diane's ex, Jim, is a total pushover...well, I guess that's not surprising. But anyway, she got him to move out and she and Todd took her old house. Jim even let her keep the kids."

"Ahhh, that's why she's back," Kate said.

"Yup," Michelle sighed. "Lucky us."

Kate and Michelle commiserated for a few more minutes before Michelle left to pick her youngest up from preschool. Kate reluctantly made the trek down the street to get Lizzie off the bus. She'd tried to time it so she didn't have to wait long but of course the bus was running late. One mother was already there and several others arrived just after Kate.

Kate tried to be polite but kept herself separate from their little group. It made her sad inside, though. She'd always enjoyed their conversations. She could see them murmuring with each other, even though she couldn't hear their conversation. She wished Doug's wife, Christine, was there but their kids went to private Catholic school.

Tension was mounting inside of her when one of the mothers called her name.

Kate turned. It was Janie, one of the moms who lived closest to her. She had two extremely rambunctious boys that were older than both her girls.

Kate smiled. "Hey, Janie." She felt her tension growing, pressing on her chest like a crushing weight on her heart.

Janie stepped over and the other moms followed but kept their distance.

"I just wanted to tell you...I was at the school today...and I heard the...*conversation* between Diane and Michelle."

Kate took a deep breath and struggled to find a response when Janie put her hand up to stop her.

"I'm just bringing it up because I thought you should know that I don't believe anything Diane said and I'm pretty sure most of the moms in there didn't either."

Kate exhaled. "Thank you," she said. "I'm assuming it was terrible."

"Shockingly so," Janie admitted. "If they hadn't already arrested that other girl, I'd wonder if Diane had something to do with it, she seemed to know so many details. But Michelle made sure everyone knew Diane was exaggerating or lying. Diane really tried to argue with Michelle but Mary Morgan backed her up and warned Diane that she'd have the school ban Diane from the property if she kept it up."

Kate was surprised. "Can she do that?" she asked, and Janie nodded energetically. The women behind her followed suit.

Janie snorted. "Mary's president of the PTA. She has a really good relationship with the school administration so I'd say yes, she definitely can do that. Anyway, I just wanted you to know we don't think you had anything to do with your husband...I mean ex-husband's murder. And we really don't want you to feel like you can't come down here and wait with the rest of us."

One of the women behind Janie stepped forward. Kate didn't know Ashley well but knew she lived closer to Diane than to Kate. Ashley held out an envelope.

"I wanted to give you this," she said. "Maddie, my youngest, is having a birthday party and she really wants Emma to come."

Kate looked down at the invitation. "Thank you. I'm sure Emma would love to come. She talks about Maddie all the time...but...I'm concerned about Emma being around...other children right now." Emma had gone to Maddie's birthday party last year, as had Diane's youngest son, Tyler. The last think Kate wanted was to expose Emma to Diane's brand of crazy.

Ashley gave her an embarrassed smile. "I understand. If it makes it any better, it's a girls- only party. Tyler won't be there....or Diane."

Kate's smile was genuine. "In that case, Emma will definitely be there." And with that, the tension drained away completely and the women all moved closer to offer Kate overdue words of condolences. By the time the bus finally came, Kate no longer felt like an outcast.

TWENTY TWO

Things in the neighborhood did get better. Following Janie's lead, more of the mothers came forward to reassure Kate that Diane's smear campaign wasn't working and that they knew exactly what she was trying to accomplish. Unfortunately, Diane still had one final confrontation in her.

Just when Kate thought everything had calmed down, Emma brought home a flyer announcing the Third Grade Chorus concert. Kate hadn't been back to the school since her disastrous effort to volunteer so she was nervous about being around all those parents. It certainly didn't help to know that Diane would definitely be there since Tyler was in the same grade.

Kate tried to put on a positive face for Emma but she was dreading it. Luckily, Michelle would be there so she'd at least have one person at her back. She wanted to ask Patrick to come but didn't need to add fuel to the gossip fire.

Kate left for church that morning, still nervous about what she was going to face that night. She had two patients scheduled and Evelyn had promised to come in, so at least she had something to distract her.

Her first patient was a referral from the diocese. It was a woman who was struggling with her daughter's desire to separate herself from her mother. Kate could tell the woman's hypercriticism and fear of abandonment stemmed from early childhood experiences with controlling parents. The poor woman was seriously challenged by her own deeply ingrained habits and was most likely facing years of therapy to help her overcome her own issues before she could even think about trying to build a healthy relationship with her daughter.

The second was Holly reporting that her attempt to avoid shopping had ended in catastrophic failure, which had resulted in several hundred dollars of merchandise from Target and an extremely angry husband. Kate reassured her that setbacks would happen and offered to work with Holly on site to determine what was driving her need to spend. They set a date and resolved to reinforce the twelve step approach to dealing with Holly's addiction.

Kate ended her day with a long visit with Evelyn. Kate enjoyed her time with Evelyn. She owed so much her from her recommendation to the church that she was happy to oblige the older woman's need for social interaction.

Kate made it home just in time to pick up Lizzie. After lunch, she settled Lizzie down with a book and wondered what to do about her youngest now that more women were calling in to the church to schedule appointments. The school year wasn't even half over, but Kate was hesitant to bring someone in to watch Lizzie in the afternoons. Annabelle had gone away to college and though the college wasn't that far away, she had no idea what the older girl's schedule was like.

By the time Emma came home, she was excited about the concert, and Kate didn't have the heart to put her cowardice over Emma's enthusiasm. They ate a quick dinner and drove back to the school. Luckily, Michelle was already there and had saved seats for her and Lizzie. Unfortunately, they were right near the front. Kate sat down and tried to be inconspicuous while Lizzie shared her activity bag with Michelle's son, Ben.

Though there were plenty of curious looks and a handful of whispers, Kate could tell that most of the parents in the makeshift auditorium either didn't know or didn't care about her history and she was fine with that. It was still incredibly uncomfortable to know that some people were still boring holes into the back of her head with their judgment. Worse, she could see Diane down at the end of the row with her only friends, Sherry and Janet. They made a great show of acknowledging her presence then ignoring it. Kate wasn't surprised that the seat next to her remained empty despite its prime location in front of the stage. Who in their right mind would want to sit next to a murderer?

Kate stared at the stage in front of her, resigning herself to her new social status as neighborhood pariah when Mary Morgan sat down next to her. Mary's husband, George, stood nearby with his video camera ready. He gave Kate a friendly wave, which she happily returned.

"You were smart to bring something for Lizzie to do," Mary remarked casually. "I had one of the high school girls on our street stay with Heather. There's no way she could sit through a whole concert."

"I'm not sure you want to sit next to me," Kate said, her comment tinged with a mixture of sarcasm and regret. "I wouldn't want to infect you with my deteriorating social status."

Mary snorted. "I'm not worried. I'd rather sit next to you than someone who sleeps with other women's husbands," she said, loud enough that Diane and her friends fell silent.

Michelle coughed out a laugh then choked. Kate could sense Diane glaring at them as she pounded on Michelle's back. Diane looked like she was winding up to return the insult when the children filed onto the stage.

Kate smiled the entire half hour of the concert and was sincerely disappointed when it was over. What they lacked in talent, the children made up in charm and the school's music teacher wisely highlighted that charm in her music choices. At the end, Kate felt a slight pang that Emma and Lizzie only had her now to enjoy the milestones of their lives.

Michelle seemed to follow her thought and gave her a sympathetic smile as the parents stood and moved toward the doors to pick up their children from the hallway outside the cafeteria. Kate had turned to follow the crowd out when she heard Diane comment nearby.

"I'm surprised her boyfriend had the balls to stay away. I'd be worried she'd cut my head off too," Diane commented. Sherry and Janet laughed nervously.

Kate was shocked. She turned and saw Michelle's mouth fall open and her eyes go wide.

If Lizzie hadn't been holding onto her hand, Kate would have laid into Diane right then and there. Luckily, Mary had no qualms.

"You do realize you're guilty of far worse than being married to a man who was killed, don't you?" Mary asked loudly, and the crowd around them fell silent, including Diane and her friends. "You think you can say whatever you want about Kate and people aren't going to remember that *you* broke up a marriage?"

Kate watched Diane's face go red. "A man is *dead, Mary.* They *investigated* her, *Mary.* They wouldn't have done that if they didn't *know* she did it," Diane answered, her words dripping with scorn.

Michelle grabbed Lizzie's hand and pulled her out of the crowd with Ben barely holding on. Kate watched them go out of the cafeteria then turned and faced her nemesis.

"They investigated everyone around him," Kate replied, fighting to keep control of her voice. She sounded calm when she really wanted to scream, "his family, his employees...everyone...even you. But they didn't arrest *you*, did they? Maybe they should have. You're as guilty as I am." Kate looked thoughtful. "In fact, you've had so much to say about the night he was murdered...maybe they *will* arrest you. Then you'll have someone like *you* on your jury, you'll go to prison anyway, and morons just like *you* will say you deserved it."

Kate felt a measure of satisfaction watching the color bleed from Diane's face. It was just as she suspected. Diane was a masterful backstabber but when confronted, she couldn't hold on to her power.

"You can say whatever you want about me, Diane, as long as it's true. But once you start making things up or exaggerating to make it sound like you know more than you do, there will be consequences. And you'd better be prepared to face those consequences."

Diane's face went through a range of expressions. When she felt like Diane finally got the message, Kate turned her back on her and walked away.

Michelle waited for her in the hallway with both Lizzie and Emma. Kate worried what Lizzie might have heard but was relieved to see her giggling with her classmates.

"Oh my God, what a..." Michelle began then remembered the children, "bubblehead. I hope you shut her up for good."

Kate's smile was tired. "Mary certainly helped," she replied.

"She needs to understand that she can't tear people down like that for fun," Mary said behind her. Kate turned.

"Thank you for that," Kate said sincerely. "That's three times now that you've stuck up for me."

Mary smiled. "I just can't stand by and let Diane do something like that...to anyone. It's insane."

"Still, it was above and beyond, and I'm grateful." Kate replied.

As a unit, the three women fell silent as Diane stepped through the doors; Sherry and Janet were nowhere to be seen. Diane glanced their way, her face scowling then stalked off to grab her son. She pulled him out of the front doors of the school without saying a word to anyone.

"Let's hope that's the end of that," Michelle said and Kate silently agreed.

TWENTY THREE

Surprisingly, that was the end of it. After the concert, Diane seemed to drop off the face of the planet. Kate learned from both Mary and Michelle, as well as from the group of moms at the bus stop, that Diane had stopped volunteering at the school and was avoiding everyone in the neighborhood. A couple of weeks later, Michelle reported that Diane's ex-husband, Jim, had grown some testicles and was forcing her to sell the house they had shared prior to their split. Smelling trouble on the way, Diane's boyfriend promptly dumped her and reconciled with his former wife. With no boyfriend to pay her mortgage and soon no mortgage to pay anyway, Diane had no choice but to leave. Though she was sure Diane expected some kind of going away party or at least a goodbye from the neighbors who still spoke to her, Diane's departure occurred quietly and without fanfare much to Kate's delight.

Kate wasn't sure which she enjoyed more as the moving truck wound its way out of the neighborhood, Diane's downfall or the fact that despite all her efforts, Diane had failed in ostracizing Kate from the neighborhood. Either way, Diane was out of the picture and it looked to be permanent. Weirdly, she was still getting texts from her mystery person and assumed it was Diane getting in a last few digs. She continued to ignore them since they were mostly benign and commented on her relationship with Patrick. Kate briefly contemplated changing her phone number but it would have been too much trouble to let everyone know what her new number was. Instead, she set her phone to auto reject the messages and put it out of her head.

What she couldn't put out of her head was her slowly disappearing relationship with Patrick. Daily texts had turned into alternate day texts, and weekly visits turned into occasional appearances. When he was around on the weekends, he was loving and attentive, but Kate felt like she was very much a nonfactor during the week. She wondered if he was seeing someone else, but since they'd never stated that they would be exclusive, she didn't feel she had the right to expect him to define their relationship.

Patrick had been unavailable the last couple of weeks citing a group project that was due so she was surprised to get a message from him that he would be coming to see them that Saturday. Her feelings about it were mixed but she messaged back that they would be happy to see him.

On Saturday, Kate and her girls waited the better part of the morning for Patrick to show up. As it grew later, Kate grew angrier and her girls grew tired of waiting. Finally, they begged Kate to let them go down to Michelle's backyard to play with their friends and Kate relented.

It was well past lunchtime when Patrick finally knocked on the door. Kate answered and her heart lurched at the sight of him standing on her front steps. His smile was guileless and charming, and as angry as she was, her disappointment faded when he stepped in and pulled her into his arms.

Kate melted against him and inhaled the clean sweet scent of him but she came to her senses and pulled away.

Patrick didn't seem to notice. "Where are the girls?" he asked instead.

"They're down playing in Michelle's yard," she answered, leading him through the house.

Patrick nodded and took a seat in the kitchen. "So what's the plan for today? You guys doing something fun?"

Kate looked at him curiously. "I thought you were coming so we could all do something together."

Patrick returned her look with one of confusion. "Oh...we were? I was just coming to check in to see how you guys were doing. I've got to go back and help my brother-in-law move some stuff out of his basement."

Kate let out a sigh. "You know, Patrick, we were waiting for you. The girls were waiting for you because we all thought you were coming to spend time with us."

Patrick looked embarrassed. "I don't remember what I said earlier. I'm sorry if I made you guys wait on me."

"That's not the point," Kate answered. "I don't want to be one of those women who complains about their relationship but...since you took the job in Potomac, we hardly see you, and when we do it's only for a couple of hours. If it were just me, it wouldn't be that big of a deal but Lizzie and Emma don't always understand why you don't come to see them or spend time with us."

Kate noticed Patrick's expression was a combination of shame and irritation that looked remarkably like one John wore on a regular basis. She steeled herself for the inevitable outburst that was sure to follow.

But Patrick surprised her. "I'm so sorry. I don't want Lizzie and Emma to feel like I don't care about them. I guess I'm not used to having that kind of responsibility. I've never dated anyone who already had a family."

His comment was very close to her biggest fear that she was keeping Patrick from experiencing the joys of starting his own family with someone he loved. She was about to let him off the hook for everything when he got up and put his arms around her.

"I promise I'll do better by you," he said. He kissed her gently. "I still have to go help at my sister's, but I want Liz and Em to know that I missed them and I'm coming back."

Kate nodded and led Patrick out the back door. They could hear the kids screaming with laughter as they made their way through the backyard to Michelle's house. Kate could see that Michelle had brought out water guns and was filling balloons with water for the kids to throw at each other. She looked up as Kate and Patrick stepped into her yard. Her neighbor stood behind her with an odd expression on her face then turned away to hand a water balloon to her preschooler.

"Patrick!" Lizzie screamed. She tore across the yard to hurl her wet little body against Patrick's legs. Emma smiled and followed but at a more sedate and leisurely run.

Patrick gave them both hugs. His shirt bore the wet imprint of little girls' bodies when they pulled away.

"Hey, pretty girls," he said. "I missed you."

"You want to be on my team?" Lizzie asked. "I throw hard."

Emma gave her sister an exasperated look. "For the last time, Lizzie, we're not playing teams."

"I can't, sweetheart," Patrick replied sweetly. "I'm supposed to be somewhere this afternoon. But I wanted to say hi and see if you guys wanted to go to Adventure Park tomorrow."

"Yes, yes, yes," Lizzie screamed and started jumping up and down so enthusiastically she broke her water balloon on herself.

Patrick smiled. "I'll see you tomorrow then, OK?"

Lizzie and Emma gave him another hug before running off to play. Patrick gave Kate a quick peck and set off back to his car.

Kate stepped across the wet yard to help Michelle fill balloons.

"That was sweet," Michelle remarked as she handed Kate the bag of balloons.

Kate nodded. She glanced at Dawn who was looking at her with an odd expression on her face. Michelle followed her look then paused in her filling.

"What?" Michelle challenged Dawn.

Dawn shrugged and tried to look nonchalant. "Don't you think it's damaging to your girls for you to be seeing someone half your age?

Kate startled and looked a Dawn more closely. Dawn's comment quoted one of the mysterious text messages verbatim.

"Patrick is only ten years younger than I am."

"Still," Dawn replied, "that's a big difference."

"Are you kidding?" Michelle asked. "Your husband is more than ten years older than you are."

"That's different," Dawn insisted. "It's different when the man is older. It's desperate when it's the woman...it's not acceptable."

Michelle looked at her, her expression incredulous.

"That's a ridiculous double standard," Michelle started but Kate interrupted her.

"You're the one that's sending me text messages, aren't you?" she asked.

Dawn blushed a deep red and turned her face away, her expression mulish.

Michelle looked thunderstruck. "She's been sending you *what?*"

Kate answered Michelle, her eyes still on Dawn. "Someone started sending me text messages when Patrick and I first started seeing each other. I thought it was John but they kept coming after he died. I blocked the number so I don't know if they are still coming."

Dawn looked annoyed at that last part. "I was just trying to save you from embarrassment. You don't see anyone else here running after a teenager like he's some toy boy plaything."

Michelle shook her head. "Speak for yourself, Dawn. If I was divorced, I would have no problem playing with Patrick's....toy," she amended as Ben ran up to have his water gun filled. "Besides, Patrick is hardly a teenager. He's a grown man. Who are we to say whether or not they should date each other?"

Dawn shook her head. "She looks desperate...like some cougar," she insisted. "It's wrong no matter what you say about it."

Michelle wasn't buying any of it. "*You* think it's wrong. It's only your opinion that it's wrong."

"Everyone thinks it's wrong...because it is. Think of the children. I'm sure they're embarrassed by all of this but they're too young to speak for themselves. And don't think everyone else isn't talking about it."

Michelle was about to continue the argument when Kate interrupted her. "Do you speak for everyone?" she asked then continued before Dawn could answer her. "No, you don't. And you don't get to tell other people how they should live their lives. What I do doesn't affect you in any way whatsoever."

"I'm not the one dating a child," Dawn answered, her tone defensive.

"Aren't you Kyle's second wife?" Michelle asked. "How do we know he was actually divorced when he started dating you? Don't you have stepchildren? Did you think about them when you started seeing their father?"

"That's different," Dawn replied, looking uncertain.

"How?" Michelle asked. "You're the Patrick in your own scenario. You dated a man who was more than ten years older than you, was married, and had children. Your situation is no different than Kate's. So why so judgy?"

Dawn's uncertainty turned to confusion. "Because it's normal for men to want to be with a younger woman..." she said, then trailed off as if unwilling, or unable, to finish her thought without sounding like a misogynist.

Michelle wasn't about to let her off. "That's amazingly hypocritical and a ridiculous double standard. You should probably rethink your position. You might realize that you are in almost the exact same situation as Kate but from the other side."

To her credit, Dawn looked ashamed. Michelle and Kate shared a glance then resumed filling balloons and water pistols.

After a time, Dawn spoke. "I'm sorry, Kate. I still think it's wrong, but it was none of my business. I shouldn't have sent those texts."

Kate stood tall and looked at Dawn. Michelle paused in her filling and glanced between the two women.

"You're right," Kate replied. "It isn't any of your business. And honestly, what you think doesn't matter to me. Unless you're going to be perfect for the rest of your life, you have no right to judge what other people do."

Chastened, Dawn nodded and quietly left Michelle's yard for her house next door.

Michelle shook her head. "What the hell? Is there something in the water?" she remarked.

"Seems like it, doesn't it?" Kate replied. She and Michelle shared another look then resumed their filling.

The next day, Patrick arrived early to take Kate and the girls to Adventure Park. It was a lovely time but Kate still felt a disconnect from him that she couldn't quite overcome. To his credit, Patrick seemed to sense her reticence and made great effort to pull her into the fun. By the end of the day, everyone was exhausted and it was with relief that Kate sent her girls to bed.

Patrick waited in the family room and patted the seat next to him when Kate walked in. She sat down facing him with her knee up, inadvertently placing a barrier between them. Patrick leaned over and took her hand.

"I hope the girls had a good time," he said quietly.

Kate gave him a wry smile. "I don't see how they couldn't. Endless cotton candy and roller coasters? I'm sure they had a great time. Thank you for taking them."

Patrick shrugged but she could tell by his small smile that he was pleased with himself.

"I should be going soon. I've got a long drive back and the beltway is going to be a nightmare."

Kate was unsurprised. She knew she should be grateful that he spent the day with them but she had hoped there would be more. She didn't know if her expectations were unreasonable or if this is what adult dating relationships were like. It had been such a long time since she was single.

"So my friend has a house in Deep Creek and I was wondering if you would like to spend a weekend there...with me," he said carefully. "The leaves should be really pretty right now and it's very quiet there this time of year."

"The water would be too cold for the girls. Are there other things to do there?" Kate asked.

Patrick looked uncomfortable. "I was thinking maybe just you and I could go. We could take the girls another time...like when it's warmer."

Kate was surprised. She'd never left the girls overnight unless it was a sleepover or it was at Michelle's house down the street. The prospect of going away with Patrick, even for a night, left Kate both excited and nervous.

"So what do you think?" Patrick asked, his thumb moving across the back of Kate's hand. "Just the two of us having a quiet night on the lake?" He looked so hopeful that Kate reluctantly nodded.

"I don't want to leave the girls for a whole weekend, but if Michelle can take them for a night...I'd love to," she replied. "But only if Michelle can do it."

Patrick gave her a flash of his amazing smile. "Deal."

Kate walked him to the front door where he stopped and gave her a long, lingering kiss that made her want to push him down on the couch and kiss him for the rest of the night.

"I'll see you next weekend then," he said quietly.

Reluctantly, she let him go.

TWENTY FOUR

Though she had lived in Maryland for more than a decade, Kate had never been to Deep Creek Lake. It was one of those destinations that the natives in her neighborhood remembered fondly and as they drove through, Kate could see why. Much of the area had been left relatively undeveloped and had retained its small town charm. As Patrick drove closer to the lake, the trees parted to reveal large lodge-like homes that Kate estimated sold in the million dollar range. She knew from Michelle that there were a handful of hotels, but for the most part, the area they were in was residential with views of the lake through the mature trees.

Patrick started to slow and turned left into a short drive. Kate stared up at the house. It was a large, older chalet that was modest compared to the huge lake mansions they passed, but it boasted wide decks that faced the water.

"We're here," Patrick said, as he brought the car to a stop. "What do you think?"

"It's lovely," Kate answered with a smile.

"There's even a pool if you want to go swimming."

"It might be a little chilly for that, don't you think?"

The interior was as old as the exterior. Kate estimated time had stopped somewhere in the 1970s. Everything was very old, but the house was clean, and it looked like some remodeling had been done within the last couple of decades. The ancient interior was redeemed by the wall of windows that faced the lake. The house sat on a narrow point of the lake, so homes opposite the water were clearly visible. But the trees were in full color, and from the deck, the view was beautiful. The lake was deserted, and the water shone like glass, reflecting the brilliant colors of the leaves and the late afternoon sky.

"Pretty, isn't it?" Patrick asked, dumping grocery bags onto the tiled counter in the kitchen. "My buddy inherited the house from his grand-dad when he passed away last year. Matt's family's been coming here forever."

"It's very pretty," Kate answered. And it was, though she had been expecting something different. With her navy father, Kate had grown up next to large bodies of water, like oceans, so her impression of a lake was a Great Lake or Lake Tahoe where they'd skied when she was younger. This was a lake on a much smaller scale, but somehow that made it more intimate of a setting, like a secret.

"You want to go pick out a room? I'll get us something to eat."

Kate picked up her bag and went upstairs to choose from the several bedrooms available. She chose the master suite at the far end of the hall that looked like it hadn't been occupied within the last few years. Kate dropped her bag onto the bed and went back downstairs.

Patrick wasn't in the kitchen. After a brief search, Kate found him outside setting up wine and cheese next to the pool. Someone had been by recently because the pool was clean, despite being uncovered and surrounded by trees. Kate wondered if the owners had been back recently during the Indian summer they'd just experienced. She sincerely hoped no one was going to show up while she and Patrick were there. She wasn't sure she could face any kind of scrutiny right now.

"I hope you like it," Patrick said, breaking into her thoughts as he fussed with the crackers.

Kate didn't know if he was talking about the house or the wine, so she simply smiled then took a seat across from him.

"I should have asked if you like red wine," he said, his tone uncertain. He seemed nervous for some reason.

"This is fine," she reassured him. "Isn't this a red blend?"

Patrick nodded and sat back to watch her. Kate stared back and marveled at how handsome he really was. His face was still tan from the summer spent outside; his skin glowed against his crisp white shirt. With the pool behind him, he looked like a fashion editorial out of an expensive men's magazine. His long fingers gently cradled his wine glass, and when he reached over to grab a cracker, she saw his hair had grown a bit and was gently brushing his collar. She felt a familiar ache grow deep within her.

"It's so quiet here," she commented just to have something to say.

"It is now," Patrick agreed. "Summertime's noisy though. Lots of kids...people on the water."

"Have you known the family long?"

"Matt's my best friend. We went to school together then we both went to College Park." Patrick looked at her, and Kate felt her heart melt. "You're going to love him. He's hilarious...funniest guy I know."

Kate smiled back, knowing it was unlikely she'd ever meet this Matt. She knew in her heart that Patrick lived in the moment and as soon as he dropped her off at her house tomorrow, she'd be off his radar for a while. It was something they needed to talk about but Kate kept stalling in the hopes that Patrick would somehow become more invested in their relationship. Michelle had urged her to think about what her expectations were from this relationship, and for some reason Kate couldn't quite figure it out. If someone asked her if she expected Patrick to marry her, she'd say no but wouldn't be able to explain why. He was sweet and extremely handsome and smart but there was a lack of intention, an avoidance or inability to plan beyond the now. With two small girls, Kate didn't have the luxury of looking at life the same way Patrick did. Everything she did had to be with the goal of providing the best possible life for her girls.

Patrick began to fidget under her stare and started to make small talk about friends and summers and the lake. Kate took pity on him and threw him a bone.

"Is there somewhere to walk near the lake? Like a path?" she asked.

"There is, but it's a few houses down. Is that what you'd like to do? Go for a walk?"

"I'd love to see the lake better."

With the turning of the fall, the leaves of the trees that lined the road were a riot of color. It was growing chilly and Kate was glad to have worn her sweater. The road was quiet as they walked along.

"There are only a few people that live here year-round," Patrick explained. "Most just come here for vacation."

Kate was impressed at that. All of the homes they passed were large and most of the newer homes were practically mansions. Between the trees she could see glimpses of the lake where it opened wide under the darkening sky. She was about to ask how far they were going when Patrick led her through the trees to a clearing that served as a public access for the homes that did not have their own docks. They found a bench at the far end of the clearing and sat and watched the sky paint itself in the pinks and golds of the setting sun. Overhead, stars made their appearance between the leaves of the trees above and the wind sent a ripple across the still water, followed by a shower of falling leaves.

Kate shivered, and Patrick put his arm around her and pulled her close. She sank into his embrace and closed her eyes to press her face against the hollow place under his jaw. She inhaled deeply, intoxicated by the sweet scent of his skin. She could feel him rest his cheek on the top of her head and wondered if his eyes were closed too.

"You know, I don't think I've ever really looked at the lake like this," he said quietly. "We're usually here when it's crowded with summer people, and we're the ones causing all the trouble."

Kate smiled, but her smile was sad. There was a canyon of years between them, and it hurt to be reminded of it.

"I can't believe you've never been here," he continued. "I thought everybody came to Deep Creek."

Kate pulled away and looked at him. "I didn't grow up here the way you did. My dad was in the Navy and we traveled a lot when I was younger. Then when it was time for me to start high school, he took a position at the base in Norfolk. When he passed away, my mother moved here to be closer to her family while I stayed in Virginia to go to college. I didn't come here until I was done with grad school and by then I'd already met John."

Patrick looked away, and Kate felt terrible bringing up her dead ex-husband.

"It is very pretty here," she commented, more to change the subject than anything else. "When my father was stationed in California, we vacationed at Lake Tahoe so that's kind of what I was expecting. But this is more intimate than Tahoe, though the homes are just as nice."

Patrick nodded again but didn't answer. It was getting dark, so they set off back to the house. Kate brought in the food and wine from the pool while Patrick pulled out the ingredients for dinner.

"Now I'm warning you," he began. "I only know how to cook like one thing so I hope it turns out OK."

Kate laughed. "Would you like me to make dinner?" she asked but Patrick shook his head.

"Nope," he answered even though he was staring at his array of ingredients with a look of concern. "I'm taking care of you tonight."

Kate's heart lurched a little. More than anything, she wanted someone to take care of her but knew deep down that Patrick wasn't that someone.

Dinner was better than Kate had expected. Since Patrick had cooked, Kate offered to clean up while Patrick sat at the counter and recounted stories of his college glory days. She was just finishing up when a door flew open at the front of the house. Kate startled and turned to see a handful of Patrick clones filing into the kitchen.

"Dude!"

Kate watched Patrick, all smiles, as he jumped up and bro-hugged the leader of the pack.

"What's up, man?" Grunts, greetings, and high fives flew around the room.

"Obendorf said you were going to be here. We came to crash your love nest," the leader announced. He took notice of Kate standing near the sink.

"Damn, Trick," he said feigning a look of shock. "Your woman is blazing." Kate blushed as he crossed the small kitchen, holding out his hand. "I'm Parker, Trick's roommate. You must be Kate. Trick said you were hot but...damn."

Kate shook his hand and smiled awkwardly. Somehow, their quiet but lovely evening had turned into a frat party. Though they sounded like forty, only four of Patrick's friends had descended upon them.

"Trick?" she asked. She gave Patrick a pointed look.

Patrick looked embarrassed. "Yeah...It's a nickname that just won't go away."

Parker snorted. "Dude, you earned that name. Don't try and play like you don't know why."

Kate waited for some sort of explanation.

"Uh, it's really nothing," Patrick stammered and his friends laughed.

"Dude, you're such a pussy," Parker remarked then turned to Kate. "Trick here's magic with the ladies but I don't need to tell you that."

Patrick blushed but he didn't deny the claim. Kate was mortified. Luckily, the group's attention span was short and they set about helping themselves to the leftovers and everything else in the refrigerator. Kate refused to play mother so she hung back and waited for Patrick to usher out his friends so they could resume their evening. Instead, Patrick settled in with his buddies and the contents of the Obendorf liquor cabinet, leaving Kate to her own devices. Seriously pissed, she watched them for as long as she could stand them, which was about a minute, then left the room and went upstairs to bed.

Hours later, Kate woke up to find Patrick asleep next to her. Mindful that the house most likely still held a handful of young men, she crawled out of bed and wrapped a small blanket around her then went out onto the deck to sit and stare at the water. Kate pulled the blanket closer as a cold breeze rippled the lake in front of her. She thought about what she wanted from Patrick. She was beginning to feel like he was functioning more out of duty to the woman he was sleeping with rather than a sincere desire to want to see her and be with her. She suspected she'd originally been a trophy fuck more than a possible relationship and that Patrick came back after John's death out of some weird sense of obligation. The idea that this was a pity relationship based on her previous troubles bothered her. Worse, it wouldn't do Lizzie and Emma any good to have Patrick flit in and out of their lives without any real consistency or commitment.

At the same time, Kate wanted to ask Patrick to state clear intentions about their future, to know what he wanted from their relationship. She knew he cared for her but they'd never had any kind of conversation about the future, if there even was a future for them. This uncertainty was making her feel off balance and needy and she hated herself for it. Her faced burned with self-loathing and not even the firm breeze off the lake could soothe her shame. Kate's eyes grew tired and her head was starting to hurt; though whether it was from her overactive anxiety over her relationship with Patrick or the noise from the impromptu after party, she didn't know.

Kate mentally said goodbye to the lake, then went back inside to sleep.

TWENTY FIVE

Kate was silent on the ride home. Patrick's friends had departed late the next morning after Kate caved and made them all breakfast to soak up the copious amounts of alcohol they'd consumed. To his credit, Patrick seemed less hung over than the others and appropriately agreed that their intimate evening had been hijacked.

The ride back seemed to take forever and she was relieved when Patrick pulled to a stop in front of her house.

"My sister, Anna, and her husband are having a housewarming party in a couple weeks and I was wondering if you would like to come with me?" Patrick ventured carefully.

Kate was caught off guard. She'd been hoping for an apology. "You mean to meet your family?" Patrick nodded. "I'm not sure that's a good idea. Won't they be a bit...taken aback?"

"I don't think so. I think they'll love you and the girls," he replied.

Kate disagreed but didn't have the heart to speak it out loud. He looked so hopeful that she reluctantly nodded.

"Sure. That would be nice." She leaned over and gave him a quick kiss and exited the car before he could say anything else.

She waved as he drove away and headed to Michelle's to pick up the girls.

Michelle's face was pensive when she opened her front door. Kate sensed there had been a problem during her time away.

"What?" Kate asked.

"Maybe it's nothing...but Emma is definitely going through something right now. I mean above and beyond what's already happened."

"What makes you say that?"

"I don't know how to describe it," Michelle said. "But she seemed short-tempered and just really, really sensitive."

Kate's heart hurt. Lizzie and Emma seemed to be dealing with their dad's death, if not well, then at least normally. The idea that she'd neglected their emotional wellbeing in any way was crushing.

"I'm so sorry," Kate replied. "Was she difficult to manage?"

Michelle led Kate down to the basement shaking her head as she descended the steps in front of her.

"No," Michelle reassured her. "She was fine otherwise. I just wanted to make sure you knew about it. It might not mean anything."

Kate found her girls watching a movie with Michelle's daughter Kelly while Ben sorted through the hundreds of multi-colored Legos scattered all over the floor.

"Mommy!" Lizzie cried. She ran to her mother. Emma slowly followed. Kate gave her a big hug and pulled Emma into an embrace. She felt Emma sink into her but that was the most her daughter was going to give her for the moment.

"You guys ready to go home?" she asked and was relieved that both girls nodded. "What do you say to Miss Michelle?"

"Thank you for letting us spend the night here and for the ice cream and the movies..." Lizzie answered dutifully and with great enthusiasm, while Emma just offered a quiet "Thanks."

Michelle smiled. "You're welcome."

Kate offered her own thanks.

"Any time," Michelle answered, "Besides, Dave and I want to do a date night soon, so I'll be hitting you up for some babysitting shortly."

"Absolutely," Kate replied, before following her girls out of the house.

Later that night, after Kate had put Lizzie to bed, she poked her head into Emma's room to see if she was still awake.

Though the lights were off, she could see Emma staring out the window next to her bed. Kate stepped in and sat down.

"Miss Michelle said you seemed upset. Do you want to tell me why?"

Emma shook her head.

"Is it because of Daddy?

Emma's face scrunched up as if she was going to cry. "I don't want to talk about it."

Kate wanted to pull her daughter into her arms and comfort her but knew Emma was starting to develop normal personal space boundaries. Instead she rubbed Emma's foot and was gratified when Emma didn't pull away. "You don't want to talk about it, or you don't want to talk about it with me?" Kate asked carefully.

Emma didn't answer for a long time. Kate waited while Emma seemed to struggle with her answer. Finally, in a quiet voice, Emma said, "With you."

Kate sighed. She was afraid of that. Then an idea hit her.

"Would you like to talk to Reverend Jess?" she offered, knowing Emma loved the tiny priest.

Emma nodded then yawned. "Can I go to sleep now?"

"Of course. Can I kiss you goodnight?"

Emma smirked a little. "Of course," she said in perfect mimicry of her mother.

Kate smiled but was inwardly sad that her baby girl was growing up. She leaned over and gave Emma a quick but firm kiss then went downstairs to send Reverend Jess an email.

Reverend Jess made time for them the following Monday afternoon. Emma was shy but took Reverend Jess's hand and let the priest lead her into her office. Kate turned, prepared to wait outside in reception when Reverend Joyce popped her head out and waved her into the library conference room.

"I wanted to have a quick word with you in private," Reverend Joyce began as she closed the door behind them. Kate felt a quick lurch in the pit of her stomach and wondered why she always felt like she was in trouble.

"Is something wrong?" she asked, taking the chair that Reverend Joyce offered.

"No. I wanted to give you a heads up about a strange call we received a while ago. It had actually slipped my mind until Jess mentioned that Emma might be having some coping issues." Kate watched as Reverend Joyce paused as if collecting her thoughts. "The caller ID showed it was a blocked number and the caller refused to give her name to reception but insisted on speaking with me." Reverend Joyce sighed and suddenly looked tired. "The gist of the caller's message was that she felt the clergy should be aware that you were involved in some impropriety that might necessitate your removal from the parish and the pastoral care counseling program. She alleged that you were sexually involved with an underage individual?"

Kate's face went hot with shame and embarrassment, but she could tell from Reverend Joyce's expression that she thought the allegation was ridiculous.

"I feel like that's not really a question but no, I'm not involved with an underage individual. I have been seeing someone casually, but he's twenty-five, not fifteen."

Reverend Joyce's eyebrows went up. "Well, I'm glad to hear we don't have an issue. The Church does not presume to interfere in the personal lives of its parishioners. If we were Catholic, though, we might have a problem," she joked then turned sympathetic. "Is this something that has the potential to become more serious?"

"I don't know. I don't think so." Kate shook her head and realized it was true. "He's a great guy but we are at very different stages in our lives."

Reverend Joyce nodded but didn't press Kate for more about Patrick. "I don't give much credit to gossips who won't give their name so I had originally decided to ignore the call, and I'm glad I did since it's a non-issue, at least as far as the church is concerned. But I am worried about someone trying to cast aspersions, if you will."

"I've already figured out who it is," Kate answered. "She'd been sending me anonymous text messages, and as it turns out, she lives just down the street from me. We've already had a conversation."

Kate felt Reverend Joyce's scrutiny and wondered what else Dawn might have said.

"You seem to be struggling with something. Do you want to talk about it?" Reverend Joyce offered.

Kate sighed. "Have you ever felt like you needed to finish something but didn't know when or how to go about it?"

"Like breaking up with someone?" Reverend Joyce guessed correctly and Kate nodded. "I've always been a firm believer that the Lord usually puts people in front of us for one of two reasons. They're either a lesson for us or a cautionary tale. Or, just to mix things up, we are that lesson or cautionary tale for someone else."

Kate's smile was rueful. "No disrespect Reverend Joyce, but I'm not sure that was helpful."

Reverend Joyce laughed. "My point is... it's up to you to determine if this relationship moves your goals in life forward, or if it's just a pleasant distraction that may or may not be contributing toward your overall wellbeing. Given the reaction of the people around you, I don't think it's difficult to see which it is."

"I think it's the latter rather than the former," Kate admitted.

Reverend Joyce looked sympathetic. "Then you probably have some thinking to do. If you need to talk it out, my door is always open."

Kate thanked her and the two women made small talk about the future of pastoral care and the possibility of bringing in more counselors. After a time, Reverend Joyce checked her watch and crossed the room to the library door to poke her head out.

"It looks like Jess is done." Kate saw Emma coming out of the office. She was relieved to see her daughter smiling. Kate was about to step forward when Reverend Joyce intercepted her.

"Emma? Would you like to come with me to see who I brought with me today?" Reverend Joyce offered and held out her hand. The Head Rector was famous for her constant canine companion so Emma smiled and eagerly took her hand.

"Kate?" Reverend Jess called from her office. Kate turned and followed the other woman in.

"I'm glad you brought Emma in," Reverend Jess said, closing the door behind her. "Even though I usually keep these meetings in confidence, I think it's important that you know what's been bothering Emma."

Reverend Jess didn't beat around the bush. "Aside from the loss of her father, Emma's feeling some guilt about her last encounter with him before he died. Apparently, there was a fight—I'm guessing between him and the girlfriend—and some words were exchanged and some things were said about you. Emma got upset and wrote her father a note before they left to return home the night on or before he died. Emma's feeling like she somehow contributed to what happened to him by writing the note."

"Did she say what she wrote?" Emma had always written notes to her whenever they had a conflict. Most of them were pleas for clemency or protestations of innocence that were far more serious than the issue itself. Kate had kept all of them and intended to give them to Emma when she was grown.

Reverend Jess shrugged. "A little and it sounds like it was relatively benign. At worst, she seems to have wanted her father to make the girl-friend stop being mean to you or she and Lizzie weren't going to stay with him anymore. It doesn't sound like anything on the surface, but because his death followed on the heels of this fight, Emma's likely feeling some guilt by association. I'm happy to keep working with her, or if you'd rather have her seen by a child therapist..."

"No," Kate interrupted. "I'll feel better if Emma meets with you. She doesn't warm up to people the way Lizzie does so it will be better for her to work it out with someone she already knows and trusts."

Reverend Jess nodded. "Then let's set a regular schedule."

Kate agreed, and the two women settled on one afternoon each week. Kate knew Lizzie would love to spend time on the playground while Emma met with Reverend Jess, so it worked out for everyone.

Kate was about to leave when Jess called her back.

"I forgot to mention it, and it might not mean anything, but one of the things that Emma was most upset about was that she saw your husband's girlfriend take—I guess it was Lizzie's t-shirt out of her bag—and insisted that it be returned since it was really your t-shirt."

Kate paused at the doorway, stunned. "Did Emma say she wrote that in the note?" she asked, her voice shaky.

Reverend Jess nodded. "Yes. Why? Is that important?"

"I don't know," Kate said, though she did know.

TWENTY SIX

By the time Kate got the girls fed, homework done and into bed, it was late. She felt badly about bothering Doug but Reverend Jess's news was too important to wait until morning. Luckily, he answered his cell right away.

Kate gave him a brief rundown of her conversation and waited as he silently considered the information she'd just given him.

"Have you seen the note?" he asked.

"No. I usually keep Emma's notes but I don't know if John would have. But since he never threw anything away when we were married, I would be surprised if he had tossed it."

Doug was quiet for another moment. "When the movers went through the condo, they only packed up the things that were to go into storage and most of that looked like personal papers. Clothes, furniture, and everything else went to ARC. I know Tim and his team went through a lot of it at the beginning of the investigation, so I don't know if the note is with the papers they took or the lot that's in storage.

Either way, they're going to want to interview Emma a little more closely now."

"Do they have to?" Kate asked. "I really don't want her to have to go through anything else."

"I agree," Doug answered. "Let me call them and see what they want to do with the information."

Kate rubbed her eyes. "I just wanted to let you know in case Bethany somehow got her hands on the note before the detectives could."

"Bethany's still in jail. The district commissioner set her bail so high she couldn't make the 10 percent. She's not going anywhere for a while." Doug said.

Kate was relieved to hear that. She worried for Emma's safety if the detectives made it known to Bethany that Emma had seen her take the shirt. She was still pondering the ramifications of this newest development when Doug broke into her thoughts.

"I have to warn you, at the very least, they're going to want to speak to Emma about the shirt," he said carefully.

Kate sighed. "I know. They might find it difficult, though. Emma hasn't been very talkative lately. And I'd want Reverend Jess there."

"I'll see what I can do. I'll give you a call later."

Kate thanked Doug and hung up.

Though to Kate the news of Emma's note was barely revelatory, to the police investigators it was big news. Once Doug made them aware of Emma's witness to the theft of the t-shirt and the note she wrote to her father, they wasted no time combing through all of the personal papers in the storage unit until they found it.

On the surface it was an innocuous note from an eight-year-old. But for the case, it was as close to a witness testimony as they were going to get. And according to Doug's friend, when they confronted Bethany with it, all her self-righteous anger and bravado finally crumbled to dust and she confessed.

Doug relayed all of this a couple of days later. Having suspected all along that Bethany was guilty, Kate was only happy that Emma wouldn't be forced to testify. With Bethany's impending guilty plea, it was now only a matter of sentencing. Unfortunately that could take up to a year or more. But it was done and Kate was relieved.

The news quickly spread through the neighborhood and the last of the Bethany defenders admitted defeat and quietly went away. Weirdly, Kate felt Bethany's confession to be somewhat anti-climactic though no less satisfactory.

Kate sent Patrick a text with the news. Michelle came over with the kids and they had an informal celebration that it was finally all over. Kate and the girls could finally move on with their lives.

It wasn't until later that night when everyone had gone home and the girls were in bed that Kate realized she hadn't heard a response from Patrick. She briefly toyed with the idea of calling him but the petty side of her won out. Kate put her phone on vibrate and followed the girls to bed.

By the next morning, Patrick still hadn't called or texted. Kate was disappointed but too distracted to dwell on it as she saw the girls off to school. She had a full day of patient appointments so she was at least able to keep busy enough prevent her from wondering about Patrick.

It wasn't late that night, when she'd reconciled herself to the reality of her one-sided relationship that Patrick finally resurfaced. Surprisingly, he was at her door and from his lopsided hello, she could tell he was a little bit drunk.

"Do you know what time it is?" she asked by way of a greeting.

Patrick swayed in the doorway. "Yeah...I'm so sorry...was at the brewery downtown and thought maybe I shouldn't drive back to Potomac right now. Can I come in?"

Kate moved aside and let him in, her expression set to hide her disappointment.

"Thank you." He gave her a slightly sloppy kiss. "The girls up?"

"It's almost eleven o'clock, Patrick. Of course they're not up."

"Oh, right." Patrick tried to give her his winning smile then stumbled a bit crossing the foyer. She followed him as he carefully navigated the path to the family room where he sank into one of her arm chairs. Kate sat across from him and watched as he tried his smile on her again. It wilted after a moment in the face of Kate's stony silence.

"Do you need some coffee?" She went to the kitchen without waiting for an answer.

"That's OK," he called after her. "I don't want you to go to any trouble for me."

She left that alone and dropped a pod into the coffee maker and waited until the cup was full. Kate brought it to Patrick and sat at the far end of the couch.

Patrick took a sip. "Thanks."

Kate could tell that as the caffeine hit him, so did the realization that he'd intruded at an improper hour.

"Oh my God. I didn't realize it was so late. Thanks again for letting me sober up. I'm not even sure how I made it over here from the restaurant."

"I guess it's better than your trying to drive back to Potomac and getting a DUI," Kate remarked then watched him take another drink.

"Did you get my message?" she asked, more to distract herself from this new mix of feelings than anything else.

Patrick shook his head through another sip of coffee. "No," he answered as he set the cup down on the table in front of him. "Did you send me a message?"

Kate leveled a look at him. "I sent you a text message that Bethany confessed. She's going to plead guilty. It's over."

Patrick's smile was sincere. "That's awesome Kate. You must be so happy."

Kate's wall crumbled a little. "I'm just glad it's done. I was hoping you would have responded to my message."

Patrick put his hand out and grabbed Kate's. "I'm sorry about that. My phone's been acting weird. I had no idea you'd left me a message."

Kate's wall had thoroughly collapsed and she returned Patrick's smile.

After another long moment of silence, Kate decided to stop beating around the bush. "Do you ever feel like 'Ugh, I've got to go call Kate now'?" she asked directly.

For the briefest moment, a look of confusion moved over Patrick's face. "No, of course not," he protested. "Why would you think that?"

"I guess when I didn't hear from you, I thought maybe it was because it...I was too inconvenient." Kate couldn't look at him. It was just too humiliating to admit her insecurity.

"Look, I'm really sorry about my phone. I would never ignore you on purpose, Kate. Please know that."

Kate chose her next words carefully. "I feel like we're not at a point in our relationship where I feel we need to be."

Patrick looked confused again. "I think I understood pretty much none of that."

"I guess what I mean is that we've never really defined what we are and where we're going with this."

"Oh." Patrick let go of her hand and sat back. "I'm not sure I've really thought it all the way through."

Kate was afraid of that. So afraid that she wasn't sure she wanted to continue with the conversation. But it was too late. She'd already planted the seed and she could see it taking root in Patrick's mind.

"I love being with you and the girls," he said carefully. "I guess I just figured things would keep going as they are. School's almost done and I have a couple of job offers here. I never really thought of having to make a plan for the future."

Kate didn't quite know where to go with that. "I guess I worry about what it will do to Lizzie and Emma if this...relationship between us doesn't last. My girls need consistency more now than ever. I can't have them feeling like anything less than a priority. I know I can't ask you to do anything you don't want to but...I guess I'm asking if this is just temporary for you."

Patrick looked sad at that last comment. "I don't feel that way. You're not temporary. I know I'm not the greatest at thinking ahead but if I had to picture the future right now, you and the girls are in it."

Kate needed more than that but she didn't want to push her luck. It was already more than he'd ever said. So she smiled and reached out for his hand again.

TWENTY SEVEN

In the wake of Patrick's late night visit, Kate had completely forgotten about his sister's housewarming party. It wasn't until he was standing on her front steps that she remembered she'd agreed to go.

"I'm sorry Patrick," Kate said. "But I didn't realize we were still going. I don't have a babysitter for the girls."

"They can come too," he answered. "My sister Caroline's kids are about the same age and I know there's going to be stuff for them to do."

Kate had her reservations about bringing her girls around Patrick's family. "I don't know if that's a good idea."

"They rented a moon bounce," he extended as incentive to let the girls go. Unfortunately for Kate, Lizzie appeared just behind her.

"I'll get Emma," she cried then ran to the back of the house.

Kate smiled. "Well, we have no choice now."

Patrick's sister's new home was only a few minutes from Kate's house in an older townhouse development in Columbia. It wasn't hard to tell which townhouse was hers with all of the children running around and the telltale moon bounce in the backyard. Kate was wary as she helped Emma unbuckle and pulled Lizzie out of her booster seat. They walked up a short set of cement steps where a small group of clean-cut husbands stood chatting over their beers.

"Hey, Scott," Patrick called. One of the men turned and smiled at them.

"Trick! What's up, buddy? Who you got there with you?"

"This is Kate, and these are her girls, Lizzie and Emma."

"Nice to meet you," Scott smiled and Kate was somewhat reassured. "Let me take you guys inside and get you some refreshments."

Patrick smiled with relief and the four of them followed Scott into the house.

Since it was an end unit, a row of windows on the unattached side let in floods of natural light revealing worn furniture and still unpacked boxes. Scott led them past a small living room/dining room combo to the open kitchen at the back of the house where a group of women (who all looked like female versions of Patrick) stood around trays of food and bottles of wine.

One of the younger women looked up. "Patrick's here," she sang. Kate and her girls hung back as the women gave Patrick hugs and made a fuss over him. After a long greeting, Patrick turned to introduce Kate and the girls.

"This is Kate and Lizzie and Emma," he stammered then gestured to the women. "Kate, meet my sisters, Anna and Caroline, and my mother...Charlotte Healey. And this is my aunt Moira."

"It's very nice to meet all of you," Kate said politely despite their barely concealed confusion. Only Anna's smile seemed sincere. "This is for you," she said, handing Anna a small basket of artisanal olive oils and gourmet salt.

"Thank you so much," Anna replied. "You're more prepared than we are. We didn't even know Patrick was bringing anyone."

Kate's face turned red with mortification. "Oh, no... I'm so sorry. We really shouldn't stay then."

"No no," Patrick's mother insisted. "You just caught us by surprise, that's all." Her smile was gracious which made Kate feel even worse. They really had no idea who she was.

Kate was about to make her apologies and leave when Megan, one of the women from her old support group, stepped through the back door.

"Kate?" Megan asked. She gave her a massive smile. "Oh my God Kate! I haven't seen you since Linda took over group. How are you?"

Kate returned Megan's smile and give her a hug. "I'm well, thank you. How are you?"

"I'm doing fine, thanks. Did you just get here? Oh my gosh, are these your girls?" Megan crouched down. "Hi there. I'm your mom's friend, Megan. Do you guys want to go on the moon bounce?"

Lizzie nodded enthusiastically as Kate demurred. "We aren't actually staying..."

"They'd love to play on the moon bounce," Patrick interjected. "Right?" Lizzie nodded with even greater enthusiasm while Emma nodded shyly.

"I'll take you guys out there," Megan offered and led Kate and her girls out the back door.

Kate followed while Patrick stayed behind.

"Jesus Patrick. A little warning would have been nice," Kate heard someone exclaim behind her. She didn't turn to look but knew Patrick was being read the riot act.

A young teenager met Megan at the end of the deck and offered to take the girls to the moon bounce where two other teenagers watched over the littler ones. Megan took charge of one of the younger kids who'd spilled something red all over himself. Kate moved out of sight of the back window but unfortunately not out of hearing of the women in the kitchen.

"I can't believe you never said anything," she heard his mother say. "I don't like how you just spring her on us like this...with no warning."

"And she has *kids*. How old is she anyway?"

"She's thirty-five," she heard Patrick answer.

"Oh my God, Patrick. Are you serious? She's my age."

"Could you just give her a chance?" Patrick replied. "She's really nice."

"I'm sure she's lovely but I really would have appreciated a little advance warning. You should have planned this better and introduced her when it was just family. How serious is this anyway?"

"Jesus, why are you all making such a big deal about this? I can't believe..." Someone closed the glass door cutting off the rest of the comment.

Megan appeared next to her, her expression sympathetic.

"So, I guess you hadn't met Anna and her family yet, huh?" she asked tactfully.

"I didn't know they weren't expecting us," Kate replied. "Patrick really should have said something. Then we wouldn't have been such an awful surprise."

Megan smiled. "Well, it was a happy surprise for me."

Kate was relieved someone was happy to see her. "So you know Patrick's family?"

"Just Anna," Megan answered. "I live just over there." Megan indicated a row of townhouses across a small open space.

"So are things going well for you?" Kate asked.

Megan nodded. "As much as can be expected. Todd's being an ass about custody for some reason. I think his mom's encouraging him to make trouble and he's hired a horrible attorney who likes her job way too much. I don't know how they're paying for her. I've heard she's insanely expensive."

"What about you? Are you represented?" Kate asked with concern.

Megan nodded. "My mom found me a really good attorney. Sort of the male equivalent of Todd's."

"So, you have family helping you then. Your mom was away for a while, wasn't she?"

"Yeah. She was taking care of my grandfather back in Korea. Since she's been back she's been a huge support. She and my dad are moving here to be closer to us so that'll make a big difference."

Kate was about to respond when Lizzie and Emma walked up. Kate could tell by their expressions that something was wrong. "I want to go home," Lizzie stated firmly, her little features struggling not to cry.

"What happened?" Kate jumped up and went to her daughter. "Are you hurt?"

Lizzie nodded but was too upset to answer.

"There's a mean boy named Brady who keeps knocking other kids down," Emma said for her. "He pushed Lizzie down and bounced so she couldn't get up." Kate glanced over at the moon bounce and saw that indeed, a rather largish boy was flinging himself about the blow up house with joyful abandon despite the obstacles of the small bodies caught inside his trajectory.

Megan stood and smiled apologetically. "I'm so sorry. Brady's extremely overindulged and can be difficult to manage. I'll go get his mother."

"I think we're just going to go now," Kate said. Megan glanced at the kitchen window then nodded her understanding. Kate moved over and gave her a hug. "It was really good to see you," she said.

Still too embarrassed to face Patrick's family again, she bid Megan goodbye and led her girls around the house back to their car. When she turned the corner at the front of the house, she found Patrick loitering with the men they had seen earlier.

"What's wrong?" he asked. "Did something happen?"

Kate closed the door on her girls then rounded on him. "Which something Patrick...the fact that your family had no clue we were coming or leaving me in a stranger's back yard while my child's being used as a tackling dummy?"

"Oh, God," Patrick replied. "Is she going to be OK?"

Kate stared at him then turned and got into her SUV. "She'll be fine. Please give your family my apologies for the intrusion."

"So I'll just call you later then, OK?" Patrick asked with a hopeful smile.

Kate leveled one last look at him and silently drove away.

TWENTY EIGHT

After the disastrous weekend, Kate was happy to go to work to deal with other people's problems. The irony that as a therapist, she was incapable of solving her own dilemma was not lost on her. She really needed to lose herself in work before she went crazy and hoped for nothing more than mild addictions, relationship issues, and general emotional distress. At least she'd have a few minutes to get herself together before her first patient. But it was not to be. Kate opened the main door and was startled to find someone already waiting for her. She didn't realize she had any appointments for the morning. Kate stepped in and wondered where Hillary was.

"I'm so sorry," Kate said as she dropped her bag onto Hillary's desk. "Did we have an appointment?"

The woman stood and smiled uncertainly then crossed the room with her hand out.

"I guess I should apologize," she replied. "The girl that was just here said I could wait to see if you were available for a walk-in."

"Sure," she replied. "I guess so. Come on in. I'm Kate, by the way."

The young woman smiled. "Elizabeth," she answered.

She was a little younger than Kate but looked familiar. Kate wondered if she was one of the mothers from the Sunday school.

"I'm not sure how things like this work," the woman said as she settled into a chair. "I guess I was wondering what exactly it is that you do for people."

"Well, in general terms, I provide pastoral based counseling, which means we will work through issues with both a psychological approach as well as faith approach."

"What kinds of issues do you normally address?" Elizabeth asked.

"Well, crisis of faith, of course," Kate answered. "I can also help with general problems like depression, marital problems, stress, anxiety...really any disorder or dysfunction."

Elizabeth looked thoughtful. "So you work with people who are having problems in their marriage?" she asked. Kate nodded. "Are you married?"

Kate knew that this question would come up at some point. "I was married for eleven years," she answered and left it at that.

"Are you no longer married?" Elizabeth asked.

Kate looked down and shook her head. "My husband left for a relationship with another woman. Then he passed away."

When she looked up, Kate saw that Elizabeth looked sympathetic. "That must have been very difficult. Do you have children?" Elizabeth asked.

This time Kate smiled. "I have two girls."

"It must have been very difficult for them...to lose their dad," Elizabeth said quietly.

Kate nodded. "It was. Luckily, we have a very loving support group both here at the church and at home but enough about me. What about you? What brings you here today?"

Elizabeth looked at her for a long moment. "Patrick's my brother."

Kate sat back surprised then wondered why she was surprised. Elizabeth looked just like him. Kate should have known.

"I know you met my family," Elizabeth said. "I'm in the middle between Caroline and Patrick."

Kate remained silent wishing Hillary would somehow know to come in and interrupt.

"Please know I'm not here to attack you," Elizabeth insisted, her tone earnest. "I'm sure it feels that way after meeting Caroline and my mother but I just wanted to talk to you about my brother."

"So, I guess you won't want me to charge you for this visit then," Kate joked. Elizabeth chuckled.

"I'm sure you think I deserve it and I'm really sorry." Elizabeth's smile was rueful and Kate found herself inadvertently responding in kind. "It's just...when Caroline told me about meeting you and how Patrick seemed to be kind of...I don't know, stringing you along sounds terrible but it's the closest thing I can think of...I thought you deserved to know all about him before you became too involved."

Elizabeth paused as if to let Kate interrupt but seemed to realize that she should continue when Kate didn't answer.

"Don't get me wrong. I love my brother but he's never been the kind of guy to assert his goals in a relationship."

"Do you mean to say he assumes a more passive role?" Kate asked even though she already knew the answer.

"Eventually, yes," Elizabeth answered. "He'll start out fully invested. He's always been the go-to guy in all his friendships and relationships but eventually, if he feels like it's too much or not exactly what he wanted, he just lets it fade away. I don't think he's ever broken up with someone. Usually girls just get tired of keeping him engaged and dump him. The ones that don't dump him just keep waiting for him to swing back around and be with them again."

"What does that have to do with me?" Kate asked, again already knowing the answer.

Elizabeth had the good grace to look uncomfortable. "If it were just you, I wouldn't stick my nose in it at all. I'd just let you figure it out. But you've got children and I'm assuming they're not that old, right?"

Kate nodded so Elizabeth continued.

"I just don't want Patrick doing his 'orbiting' thing with someone who has children. I work with special needs kids and I know how important consistency is. Your girls don't need anyone coming in and out of their lives on a part-time basis. And that's all Patrick will do, if he hasn't already."

This time Kate looked uncomfortable. "He and I have already had that conversation." Kate admitted.

Elizabeth looked at her sadly. "I'm so sorry."

Kate shook her head then smiled. "Well, is there anything I can help *you* with?"

Fortunately for both of them, Kate's first actual patient had arrived so Elizabeth made her apologies for her intrusion and left. Luckily Kate's day was full and it wasn't until much later that she could fully process all she'd learned from Patrick's sister.

But honestly, there wasn't much to think about. She'd entered into a relationship, at least as she considered it, with someone who was at a completely different stage in their life and she knew she needed to break it off.

By the time she got home and picked up Lizzie, she had resolved to call him to set up a time when they could talk face to face. As luck would have it, Patrick had heard from his sister and had shown up at the house in a snit that Elizabeth had gone behind his back.

"I can't believe she did that!" he ranted. Kate ushered a concerned looking Lizzie into the family room and parked her in front of the latest Disney DVD.

"It doesn't matter," she lied. "She's just looking out for your well-being."

"This is hard enough without my sisters getting their panties in a twist about something that doesn't have anything to do with them."

"What's hard enough?" Kate asked.

Patrick made a vague gesture between them. "Us...this...all of this. I can't jump through hoops trying to do everything right if I have my stupid sisters stirring shit up too."

"You feel like you have to jump through hoops for me?"

"Not like that," Patrick sounded irritated. "I know I screwed up by not telling them I was bringing you but I didn't think it was such a big deal. I'm not used to having to be so careful all the time."

Kate felt a wave of calm move through her. "Then don't worry about it. Don't worry about us. I don't want this to be something that's too difficult for you."

Patrick looked at her closely, his expression wary. "Seriously?"

Kate nodded. "Seriously. I'm not the mess you need to clean up. In fact, you are completely absolved of any and all responsibility to me and my girls."

"Are you sure?" he asked. "Wait, what do you mean by absolved?"

Kate chose her words carefully. "Listen, Patrick. We are in two very different places in our lives. I've already lived through all of the things you're experiencing now and things you have to look forward to. I can't go backward and try to fit into your world and I can't ask you skip past major life experiences and live in mine. It's just not going to work."

Patrick's face took on a stubborn expression. "I don't want us to break up."

"I don't either," she said gently. "But we're just too far apart in our lives. You need to experience those firsts that I've already had."

"Then I'll catch up," Patrick insisted. "Just let me get through the next few months and then we'll both be on the same page."

Kate sighed. "I don't think so."

"Seriously Kate. Please? Let's just take a break. Not a forever break but a temporary one until I get my shit together."

Kate sighed again. "Fine. But not just a couple of weeks or a month. Take your time to decide what you want. Take a year. Then if you still want this," Kate made her own vague gesture between them, "you can come back and we'll figure it out."

Patrick pulled Kate into his arms and buried his face in her hair. "I'm going to come back, you know," he promised. Kate inhaled the fresh scent of soap and sun on his skin. When he pulled away, she was surprised to see his eyes were wet.

"One year," he promised. "I'll be back."

TWENTY NINE

One Year Later:

It was another weird fall day in Maryland with temperatures rising well into the eighties before the winter's first frost. Kate hoped to get the remainder of John's things packed up before the donation truck arrived to pick it all up. She'd been staring at his tools and sports equipment for over a year and it was time for it to go. She was in the garage taping the last of the boxes up when she heard the mailman drive up. Tired of tape and cardboard and dust, Kate walked down to pick up the mail. As she walked back up to the house she sorted through the stack of flyers, sales notices and bills. Kate stopped at the recycling bin, ready to toss in the junk when she spotted a creamy white envelope. Curious she tore it open and found a wedding invitation...Patrick's wedding invitation... with a note.

Dear Kate,

I wanted to tell you before you heard about it from someone else but I didn't know how. I met a girl and I've asked her to marry me. I think I love her because she reminds me of you and I know how bad that sounds but even though I'll never admit it to her, I wanted you to know the truth. I'm sorry I'm not doing this in person but I think if I saw you again I would never leave. I was upset when you sent me away that last time but now

I understand why. I think the worst part is not being able to share those first with the person I loved the most and I hope you agree. I'll miss you and the girls but I know this is for the best.

I'll understand if you don't come to the wedding. I just wanted you to know. Please give the girls hugs and kisses from me but don't tell them it's from me. That'll just upset them. Just love them knowing how much I miss them. And you.

Love, Patrick.

Kate couldn't cry. She knew this was what was right even if a small part of her had wished he'd come back. Well maybe more than a small part but all of her understood that he deserved better than an already lived life. He deserved all that life had to offer and now he would have it.

She put the note back in the envelope then placed it in a box of books and papers that would be going into the storage unit with the rest of John's personal papers. She sealed the box with a strip of tape then went inside to give her girls a kiss.